FE05194

FX
UPDEGRAFF, R

GUIDEPOSTS

CHURCH CHOIR
MYSTERIES™

The
Kidnappers
Club

Roberta Updegraff

Guideposts®

CARMEL, NEW YORK 10512

www.guidepostsbooks.com

www.guidepostsbooks.com
Guideposts Book & Inspirational Media Division
Series Editor: Michele Slung
Cover art by Stephen Gardner & Edgar Jerins
Cover design by Wendy Bass
Interior design by José R. Fonfrias
Interior cat illustrations by Viqui Maggio
Typeset by Composition Technologies, Inc.
Printed in the United States of America

Acknowledgments

IN A WHIRLWIND FEW MONTHS, I served with my family in a small mountain village in Honduras, helped launch the ultimate road trip (yes, Mark drove the bus from Pennsylvania to Honduras), returned to substitute teaching, entertained several sets of international guests and finished this book. None of which I could have accomplished without all the wonderful support folks in my life.

Hugs to my darling husband Mark for running umpteen errands, taking over the taxi service and, most of all, giving me lots of encouragement (the massages were great, too). Kisses to Katie (our youngest and only child still at home) for being a good sport about getting forgotten or picked up late. *Abbracci* to our exchange student Dario Recalcati for all the pick-me-ups—cups of coffee and Italian cookies appearing at my computer just when I needed a break.

Kudos to my great editors at Guideposts Book and Inspirational Media Division! Managing editor Elizabeth Kramer Gold extended grace when I accidentally missed my deadline. Michele Slung does a great job making my manuscript read better, and Stephanie Castillo Samoy is always cheery—it comes across even in e-mail.

1

"THEY NEVER RECONCILED their bank statements," Jess Horton told Gracie, "so they didn't notice the six hundred dollars deficit. Can you imagine? They don't even have a clue as to how the shortage occurred!" Jess threw her hands up in the air. "But they want me to make things all right! I'm not a miracle worker!"

Gracie shook her head sympathetically. Although she and Jess had only recently made each other's acquaintance, Gracie felt a kinship with this newcomer to Willow Bend.

Jess Horton was the new feature editor at the *Mason County Gazette*. Although Gracie's friend Rocky Gravino was the eternal pragmatist (which she had to admit was a good character trait for a newspaper editor), he also had a soft spot for stray animals, kids—and now, it seemed, struggling young widows. Perhaps it was because he, like Gracie, understood the difficulty in carrying on after losing a beloved partner.

"How much money are we talking about?" Gracie focused on the problem at hand. It was hard to imagine that a band of stay-at-home mothers could amass a fortune dabbling in the stock market.

"A lot."

Gracie's eyes widened.

"Let's just say, since I don't want to be indiscreet, that they've almost doubled their investment."

Gracie gave a soft whistle.

"And they were mothers of toddlers, no less," Jess added.

Gracie remembered the young women starting their group five or six years earlier. She'd been impressed with their determination to learn about investments and the world of finance all on their own.

"Marilyn Clayton told me that in the old days the group took turns hosting the meetings in the afternoon at each other's homes," Jess explained. "The kids brought sleeping mats like they do in kindergarten, and after they were put down for an afternoon nap, the women studied the stock market."

"Now, *that's* a creative use of nap time!"

"Makes their name all the more appropriate: the Kidnappers Club."

Gracie chuckled, remembering that merry band of moms and kids in the park years earlier. She could still picture the young women keeping an eye on the sandbox, where their gaggle of preschoolers built elaborate castles and raced miniature cars on sand tracks bordered by muddy moats, emblazoned with twig-and-gum-wrapper flags.

The mothers group had invested in the future, all right, but Gracie decided that their impressive stock portfolio was probably the lesser of their successes. Those cute toddlers had matured into a great bunch of adolescents, many of whom were members of Eternal Hope's youth group.

"I admire their entrepreneurial spirit," Gracie told Jess. "In my day it wouldn't have occurred to us. But I was happy to trust my husband with all the managing of our finances."

She sighed, the ache of loss suddenly with her afresh. Jess nodded in empathy. They stood quietly a long minute, each lost in recollection. Gracie knew from Rocky that Jess had moved to Willow Bend and taken the job at the *Mason County Gazette* after her husband's recent death.

"When my husband died," Jess began, "I had two kids to think about, and all we had was his insurance money. We hadn't planned on cancer."

Gracie sought her gaze, allowing her understanding to enfold them both. *Dear Lord, how quickly grief can come crashing back. Hold on to her, Father, don't let her founder in sorrow's undertow.*

"I know the struggle," Gracie assured her.

Gracie hoped to lessen the woman's grief by sharing a story about herself. "Our son was grown with a wife of his own when El was killed. But Arlen stepped into his father's size thirteens like they were made for him. Arlen turned into more than a son—he became a good friend. Still is."

"You only have one child?"

Gracie nodded. *"And* one fantastic grandson. Little Elmo is the spitting image of his grandpa. El would have been tickled pink over his namesake."

"Bobby is named after his dad," Jess told her. "And R. J. *was* thrilled when I suggested we name him Robert John Horton the Third."

She paused. "Bobby was only four when his dad died, Molly just a toddler. I don't know if they'll remember him."

"They will, especially if you help them. Reminisce together. Kids seem never to get tired of hearing stories about their parents and grandparents."

Gracie recalled Elmo's fascination with the grandfather he'd never met, the man to whom his own dad was once a beloved little boy.

"How did your husband die?" Jess asked.

"Car accident. Rainy night . . . country road. El apparently lost control on a curve. . . ." Gracie hated remembering that fateful evening. She still could not believe it had happened. El had always been so careful! It had been an almost unendurable ordeal, but Gracie had trusted God for comfort then

8

as she did now. Looking at Jess, she felt the Lord's arms around them both.

"But, listen, this isn't solving your problem." Gracie disliked feeling sorry for herself. "Let's see if I understand correctly. You joined the group three months ago."

Jess nodded.

"But you just took over as treasurer last month."

"No one wanted the job." She gave a sheepish grin. "They've been really only doing nominal bookkeeping at their meetings, and so the books have never been audited. I made that my first priority. I used to help my husband write grant proposals, and we had to pay attention to details.

"R. J. was a researcher in the lab of a somewhat absent-minded professor at the university back near our home. Neither of them enjoyed bookkeeping, and so it fell to me by default. Carroll—Dr. Samuels—never married. R. J. was like a son to him, and I a daughter-in-law. He's a lovely man and we both adored him, but he had no sense for ledgers. Formulas, yes—account books, no." Jess laughed, remembering. "Anyway," she continued, "I've always had a knack for catching discrepancies, for want of a better word. A sixth sense, if you will, for spotting something off kilter."

"Good trait for a reporter."

"I'm really better at editing. Like I said, I'm a detail person by nature. I was an English major in college—by default, as well. I had no idea what to declare, but my father was an

English professor. My mother worked as an editor for a local publisher. So I guess I just fell into a career instead of choosing one."

Jess smiled before she continued. "Until I had children, that is. I wanted to be home, so I started helping R. J. when the children were babies. Carroll—Dr. Samuels—was only too happy to pay me. Keeping their account books kept me in spending money and close to my husband."

But there were present matters to clear up. "So," Gracie said. "You went over everything and found a six hundred dollars discrepancy, which you brought to the club's attention."

"Well, yes and no. I told Marilyn Clayton, my next-door neighbor, and our president, Darla Knight. She really didn't want to hear about it."

"It seems like it's now in her hands. I don't know what else you can do—or me, for that matter."

"Nothing, I suppose." Jess sighed. "I guess I just needed to talk it out with someone. I feel uncomfortable being put in this position. . . ."

Gracie sought the other woman's gaze. "I sense there's more to it. Perhaps something you're not telling me."

"Not really." Jess shifted her weight. "I just don't like being the bearer of bad news. Darla is sure it's just an oversight and has tried to laugh it off as sloppy bookkeeping. She suggested I re-figure the bank balance from the beginning.

But, Gracie, that makes me uncomfortable. I don't want to be blamed later!"

"Perhaps we can unravel the mystery," Gracie decided. "Let's hope it *is* just a bookkeeping error."

Jess wrinkled her brow.

"You seem doubtful at the possibility it was an honest error," Gracie ventured.

"At first, it seemed possible. We all know," Jess reasoned, "computing errors happen."

"What changed your mind?"

"It just doesn't add up, when I take into account the total number of investors and the number of months they have been contributing. I don't want to confront this until I'm sure. Darla told me to start fresh with the bank balance. That would be the easiest thing, but I really don't want to do that."

Gracie could understand why. This situation was made for trouble. She studied the woman in front of her. Jess was still frowning. It was clear to Gracie she didn't need another complication in her life.

Lord, I want to help her. Where do I begin?

"Maybe *you* could help me take a look at the books," Jess suggested, as if reading Gracie's mind. "I still have them at my house. Marilyn Clayton knows what's going on, so maybe the three of us could put our heads together one day this week."

Gracie told her that she would check her schedule and call later that evening. "First, I'd like some understanding of the group. You say *no one* kept the books before you arrived."

"Lackadaisically describes it best. Everybody admits that the group was a bit casual when it came to keeping track of who actually contributed what. In the beginning, they didn't keep any record at all, other than the monthly bank statement. They were all friends, so they were more interested in fellowship than financial accountability. And not just a fellowship but also a learning experiment. Each month they simply accepted the balance on their bank statement. Since they had so few investments, mental bookkeeping sufficed. But over the years, they began to accumulate a nice portfolio. I think that's where the problem lies."

Jess pointed to herself. "Me, I can't be so nonchalant. I'm very careful with money, especially when it isn't mine. I told Darla that I would have to resign if we didn't confront the problem. She asked me to give us some time to look into it together. But I don't know—it doesn't *feel* right."

"If there *is* something truly amiss," Gracie said, "then it's important to find out sooner rather than later."

"That's where I thought you could help. I took on this job for the sake of friendship. I've done it before, been treasurer for the Girl Scouts and for our bowling league—but there were never any problems. I really didn't expect to run into one here—not in an investment club!"

Jess looked up with steady resolve and went on, "Rocky sings your praises. And he says you're wonderfully intuitive. These women know you. They may resent my pursuing this. I'm already feeling some tension with Darla."

Even church people were touchy about finances. El had always maintained that a person could read another's heart from his check register. One only had to look where money was spent. Then there was no mystery.

"Darla was put off by my suggesting an outside audit," Jess told her. "She didn't come right out and say it, but I felt she resented my looking into the matter."

"So, you *did* suggest they get outside help. Doesn't that establish your good faith? It seems like you've done your best."

"Darla doesn't see it that way! She's defensive, as if I were pointing a finger at her. Right now, I feel like giving up— turning over the books, and telling them that I don't need the aggravation. And I don't!"

Gracie sighed. But then Jess smiled. She shrugged off her anger and said, looking earnestly at Gracie, "I really want to learn about investing. My husband's strengths lay elsewhere. Money wasn't important to him. At least we *did* have life insurance—enough to provide for our children's educations. But I've got to be careful, and invest what I do have wisely."

"Marge and I have been toying with starting one of those groups," Gracie thought out loud. "And I've been meaning to call Phyllis Nickolson. I said I'd stop by with my recipe for teething toast. Her daughter Katie and the Knight girl are friends, I think. I'll start there and see what I can find out."

Jess thanked her, looking genuinely relieved at Gracie's willingness to get involved.

"Let's pray it is just a mistake in bookkeeping," Gracie said, trying to keep her attitude positive. "And, until we know something for sure, try to put it out of your mind. You already have enough to worry about, with two young children."

Jess agreed, and shared with Gracie her fear that Bobby was having difficulty in first grade. It seemed he was becoming a bit of a bully. Molly loved her preschool, but always put up a fuss when Jess dropped her off.

Gracie could only sympathize, sending a prayer heavenward on the young mother's behalf. "It's tough being both mother and father."

An idea for help came to mind! "Does your church have a singles group? Or a support line for young parents?"

Jess's reply was curt. "I'm not interested in that kind of thing. My children come first, and my free time's reserved for them."

Gracie didn't press further. There was plenty of time to show Jess how a church family could be a real lifeline. They'd been there for her with loving hearts when El died. She couldn't imagine going on without them, especially the choir. They had become like a family: brothers, sisters and adopted children.

"Rocky wants to improve the weekend edition," Jess told her. "Provide a little more food for thought when our readers have a bit more time to think, he says. He wants me to line up a few pastors to do a weekly inspirational column, so I'm working on that now."

Gracie was proud of her old friend for trying something that went so much against his nature. The *Mason County Gazette*'s editor was unabashedly agnostic, it was true, yet Rocky had never been totally closed to the subject of religion. She had seen how his ink-stained cynicism had from time to time been at war with his secretly sentimental nature.

Rocky and El had been good friends, so it had seemed only natural that after Elmo's death that he would become her protector and confidant. And her dependence on him over the years since her husband's death had grown into a comfortable friendship. If only Rocky shared her faith! That had been something El longed for as well.

Oh, Lord, guide my reluctant journalist to listen to his heart. And comfort this young woman in all her challenges. Then show me how to help You bring them back to Your loving protection.

"Have you talked to our pastor at Eternal Hope?" Gracie decided that Pastor Paul might be just the man to draw Jess and her family back into the fold.

The younger woman's expression was suddenly cautious. Then, sensing no pressure on Gracie's part, she allowed herself to relax. She laughed. "Rocky has already suggested your minister. He's having a great time teasing me. Tall, blond and handsome, right? Perfect match."

"Rocky cuts to the chase, that's for sure."

All things considered, Rocky might actually be not so far off. Gracie looked forward to needling her old friend about playing Cupid. She was going to get at least a few good teasing moments out of this discovery, that was for sure!

Jess sensed Gracie's affection and playful spirit. "I told him to watch his step, or I was going to fix him up with the widow in advertising!" she announced, winking.

They both giggled.

"Seriously, Gracie, I've thought about joining a church. The kids and I have even visited a couple. But, I guess with what happened to my husband, we're just a little God-shy."

Gracie couldn't imagine life without Him. But she, too, knew disappointment. God didn't always answer prayer in the way one expected. Yet He'd been faithful. His way was always the right path.

"I know it can be difficult to make sense out of life." Gracie met the rueful gaze of her new friend. "I've lashed out at God when I've been hurt and angry, yet He's always been there, patiently waiting to comfort me when I was ready. It's just that we're too quick to blame God for anything that goes wrong."

"Okay, I *did* call your pastor," Jess admitted. "Paul and I are meeting tomorrow. He seems genuinely excited about doing a column for the newspaper."

Gracie was delighted. Paster Paul's sermons were full of practical applications for life. And he was an excellent shepherd, gently prodding the most obstinate of cynics to trust again, while quietly encouraging the wounded and broken sheep to stay the course. Paul could be just the friend the Lord had in mind to help this wounded but healing woman.

Lord, let us be a shining example of Your love. Fill us with Your Spirit, as we reach out to Jess and her two children. Guide Paul in the way that he should minister to this family.

She sneaked a smile skyward. *And a little romance wouldn't hurt, Lord. I think they could both use it. Our shy pastor may need help in that department. Maybe You could give him a little nudge.*

ADMITTEDLY, GRACIE wasn't fond of shopping. (Fresh fruits and vegetables were excepted, for to her nothing was more pleasing than a firm, plump eggplant or a fancy selection of fresh mushrooms.) More than anything else, she *hated* malls.

Antiseptic was the word that came to mind. There was that smell—really a certain feeling to the air, not medicinal, but calculated to create a perfect environment to separate a shopper from his hard-earned cash. She resented the relentless alluring products, inviting sales and special promotions for things she didn't need, or really even want.

A few of her friends spent a couple of mornings a week power-walking these halls. They claimed it was excellent for both socializing and exercise. But how fake plants and an artificial climate could compete with the sunlit beauty of Willow Bend's streets, Gracie simply couldn't imagine. She loved walking, but her own cozy neighborhood was the best landscape in which to do it.

As she passed each house, Gracie would lift the residents' name to the Lord in prayer. It was not unusual for neighbors to call her over to report some wonderful blessing or special opportunity that had come their way on the very day Gracie knew she had prayed for them. For her, the extra power in her walking was the power of prayer.

As she strode along, she would silently thank God, sharing His joy in quiet companionship. God was always working on their behalf; yet so often, He was taken for granted, unnoticed. So much like the good parent. And, often, the miraculous was passed off as serendipitous. Miracles were not coincidence. God was humble. He simply had no need to take credit.

She sighed. How much they could accomplish together without the need for accolades. *We could all take a lesson from You, Lord.*

Gracie thought of those Willow Bend friends and acquaintances she had prayed for over the years during those prayerwalks. They had come a long way, she and the Lord. What had begun as an exercise in grief management had become precious solace. She couldn't imagine a morning without a walk with her Creator.

But I could do the same here in the mall, couldn't I, Lord? I can pray for these shoppers. Even if I don't know them by name, You do. Together, what special blessings can we impart! She smiled inwardly, looking forward to what God would reveal this day.

As Gracie prayed a blessing for the fellow shoppers she passed, she smiled at them, and they returned the gesture. So she decided the mall wasn't such a bad place, after all. Perhaps when the weather turned cold, she might even drop in again to take her morning constitutional.

This day, she needed a new pair of pumps, and Avery Mall was the only place that had a decent selection. Marge Lawrence had offered to come along, but Gracie had been afraid her best friend would coerce her into buying something less serviceable than she preferred. Her friend tossed practicality to the wind at the sight of red patent leather, or fake alligator-hide, neither of which Gracie could imagine on her own feet.

Her son Arlen often teased that Gracie's preference for traditional styles and Marge's taste for the outrageous kept both women fashionable. Her daughter-in-law Wendy would laugh, saying that Marge's spontaneity and Gracie's practicality gave them the best of everything: a sense of adventure tempered by caution. They had had a lot of fun together, Gracie smiled in appreciation as she walked on. Lost in her thoughts, she gave hardly a glance to the display windows she passed.

Loud voices suddenly drew her attention to a middle-aged couple quarreling about finances, and she lifted them up in prayer. A solitary old man toyed with a half-melted cup of ice cream. She greeted him, saying softly, "God bless you." The shoe store she was headed for lay at the other end of the mall.

"Jim!" Gracie now greeted one of her favorite former Sunday school students.

Jim Thompson glanced around, putting a finger to his lips.

"What's going on?" she whispered, following his gaze to the group of youths standing nearby.

"I'm on duty," he said quietly. He motioned for her to join him behind the foliage in the center-court planters.

The Willow Bend policeman was not in uniform, and Gracie wondered why. She glanced around, looking for the suspect.

Two women in jogging suits chatted amiably just on the other side of the planter. Nearby the elderly man with the ice cream had stopped to talk to a young woman with a child in a stroller. Neither looked criminally minded.

"Your beat is in Willow Bend, I thought." She looked puzzled.

He motioned toward a group of kids loitering near, outside the entrance to the mall. "Potential troublemakers."

A gaggle of fashionably dressed teens laughed and joked, oblivious to official surveillance by the law. Several sported braces, and two wore ponytails—hardly the profile for juvenile offenders.

Gracie eyed him incredulously. "They don't look sinister. Why, they could be Willow Benders!"

"They *are* Willow Benders. The county sheriff called Herb." Gracie looked respectful at the mention of her friend and Jim's boss, Willow Bend's police chief Herb Bower. "Seems the department needs our help. The mall management is complaining about kids being dropped off unchaperoned. Store owners suspect some of them of shoplifting."

"Shoplifting!"

"I'm afraid so," Jim said. "It's gotten to be quite a problem. There are suspects—some teenagers—but no one has been caught red-handed. They travel in packs, creating a diversion, so it's difficult to monitor them. One kid will monopolize the clerk, while the others handle merchandise. It's almost impossible to figure out just which one is the thief."

"But the mall has security for that!"

"Surveillance isn't our job. We're just here to establish a presence." Jim smiled. "A little preventative medicine, if you will. We volunteer for this tour of duty."

Jim Thompson had a knack with kids. Gracie recalled his rapport with a group of boys for whom she had a special affection. Gracie made a mental note to check in on Chuckie, Quasi and Martin.

Jim motioned toward another group of teens just entering the mall. "This place is the most popular local hangout for Avery kids and Willow Bender ones alike. They team up with friends, roaming around, loitering, sometimes just by their presence intimidating older customers. It's a matter of the potential for mischief, as well as the fact of it."

"Where are their parents?" Gracie wanted to know.

"I guess too busy to read the signs saying that their kids actually need more supervision and guidance than they're being given."

"Perhaps you should send them home."

"Probably, but teenagers are the biggest spenders. These stores have targeted them. They've contributed to the situation. They want the profits, but not the problems. They don't want to forbid the kids coming alone because they don't want to lose money. So, I guess if parents won't take responsibility, it's up to us. As if policemen didn't have better things to attend to."

Gracie couldn't understand this reality. Parents dropped children off at the mall for a day of unsupervised shopping—but how did they even know their kids remained there? Perhaps that was the problem; no one noticed, and no one cared what teenagers did.

Things had certainly changed since her childhood—and Arlen's for that matter. Gone were days when young people congregated at neighborhood parks, playing endless games of four-square and wiffle ball. Would this be adolescence for Elmo? She prayed not.

"Things have changed, Gracie." Jim sighed. "Seems that, now, we're babysitters."

"Will you arrest anyone?"

"We're hoping a police presence will work to keep them honest. Most of these Willow Bend kids know me by sight."

"They look like such nice kids."

"Appearances are deceiving. That little group of teenage girls over there is suspect. They're here pretty regularly, and they frequent stores that have reported missing merchandise." Jim leaned close. "One of them is the Nickolson girl. I talked to Terry about her, but he's reluctant to do anything. There's tension, him being her stepfather and all. We're good friends, Terry and I, so I hate to press the issue."

He turned toward Gracie. "You're pretty tight with her mother, Gracie. Maybe *you* could talk to her. I'd hate to see a Willow Bender get into trouble. Katie's a good kid, underneath it all, and Terry's making every effort, I know."

Gracie nodded, still unable to take it all in. Respectable girls got into trouble, she understood. Nothing is guaranteed, she knew well enough from reading the papers and watching television. But the daughters of her friends and fellow citizens shoplifting? It just didn't seem possible.

"They seem to have everything."

"They probably do." Jim sounded frustrated. "That's the problem, Gracie. Parents are trying to trade *things* for *time*. These kids wind up stealing for thrills. Nothing is exciting enough anymore. What's new one minute is old—and boring—the next."

She frowned. "So, what do we do?"

"Gosh, I don't know. I've been trying to figure that out myself." He sighed. "I'm no shrink."

She looked at him in sympathy. But her heart was heavy.

"I don't want to see these kids get into trouble. The way I figure it I'm not only a police officer, but one of God's 'prayer warriors.' So I'm here, and I'm praying for them, as well as praying they keep out of trouble."

Gracie couldn't help but smile.

"The sheriff figured it might help to have local presence— a deterrent, if you get my drift. Me, I figured I'd play the 'good cop' role, warning the kids that the authorities here are tough on shoplifters. Figured that was the best approach. I introduce myself to kids, chat with the ones I already know. Get acquainted with the ones I don't. Maybe even invite them to church—our youth group. 'Officer Jim,' that's me. Maybe I can keep them on the straight and narrow. That's what I pray for, anyhow."

Gracie was thankful for his sense of duty above and beyond what was called for in his daily job. "I wish there were more police officers in our community like you," she said. "Or any other community, for that matter."

"Thanks, Gracie," he said, watching the group of young teenagers.

Gracie's gaze rested on Katie Nickolson. The girl had been navigating turbulent family waters. There had been stresses, Gracie knew, after her mother's remarriage and baby Darren's appearance. Katie had felt threatened and behaved in ways that signaled her need for reassurance.

But it seemed that, lately, there had been calmer times in the Nickolson household. Gracie recalled Phyllis's telling her that Katie had been doing well in middle school. She was making friends, and becoming more involved in clubs and after-school activities.

Shoplifting? Gracie still couldn't believe it.

"Terry says Katie is a handful, often more than Phyllis can handle with the new baby and all. It's probably easier to drop her off here than to deal with her at home."

He looked at Gracie. "But I know she respects you. Seems maybe God put you here in this place, at this time, for a reason. A little grandmotherly regard couldn't hurt."

Gracie nodded. "You really don't think Katie would do anything dishonest, do you?"

"It takes guts to go against the flow. Teenagers aren't known for their individuality. These kids travel in packs, Gracie. There's usually a ringleader, and not much argument from the rest."

Gracie hated to acknowledge the truth in that. "There's always the chance these kids will listen to the inner voices of their consciences when they're at a real crossroad. They do come from good families . . ."

Jim raised an eyebrow. "Depends on what you mean by good."

Gracie bit her lip.

"The owner of Best Friends Boutique thinks that she's the ringleader," Jim now said, pointing to a petite blonde teen whose wrists were heavy with charm bracelets.

"She's smooth. Always surrounded by other girls. Somehow, the store owner gets left holding an empty hanger."

Gracie listened and made no comment.

"They *do* make purchases," Jim conceded. "So, store owners can't very well refuse them entrance. And, of course, nobody wants to single out certain kids with no proof."

"What can we do?" The situation was confounding. Gracie couldn't see a solution, short of running a real babysitting service—and these kids were much too old. Perhaps Pastor Paul might have an idea. She made a mental note to talk to him about it.

"*You* could warn Phyllis." Jim was adamant. "Tell her that Katie's running with the wrong group. I tried, but Terry's afraid to confront her. She needs someone to run interference for her—and that someone might be *you*, Gracie."

But Gracie needed time to think and pray about what would be the best course of action. She turned to look at the girls again, wondering how she could help.

"I'll look out for our Willow Bend kids the best I can," Jim assured her. "We're family. But I can only try to keep them out of trouble. The problem is, Gracie, if they insist on getting into it, the rules of law will take precedence."

3

SPYING A MAN precariously perched on the peak of her roof, Gracie panicked, and scurried to the back of her house. As she rounded the side, she heard her uncle's voice.

"That's it! Okay, okay!" He was watching Rocky Gravino struggle with a small satellite dish.

"A jerk to the right," Uncle Miltie was shouting. As Rocky attempted to comply, the octogenarian waved a cane wildly. "Too much! Back to the left!" When Rocky made the adjustment, his overseer corrected, "No! Left! Forty-five degrees! Right—no, no, I meant *right!*"

"For Pete's sake! Make up your mind!" Rocky growled.

"Now, now, no need to get testy." Uncle Miltie's tone was contrite. "The manual says to angle it toward the largest cities."

Gracie smiled. The pair of combative gents was obviously engaged in another one of their possibly ill-fated do-it-yourself projects. "What on earth—or, should I say, under heaven—are you two doing, anyway?"

Uncle Miltie explained patiently, "Remedying our reception problems, my dear."

"I don't remember our having reception problems," Gracie told him. "The television picture seems pretty clear to me."

"You are *always* complaining about the lack of selection!" he defended.

"It's not the selection," she reminded him, "it's the quality of what's on that bothers me." She narrowed her gaze. "I don't watch enough TV to care about reception, or programming."

Rocky called from above, "The answer is, there was a sale! And we're not even going to go there, Gracie! I told him you get what you pay for, which this little gizmo is proving first hand."

Uncle Miltie clunked his cane dismissively. "It was an undeniable bargain. And we've saved a bundle installing it ourselves."

The newspaper editor snorted, "We? I don't see anyone *else* up here."

"You're going to break your neck!" Gracie called up to him. She screened her eyes, feeling terribly anxious for her friend. "You come down from there this instant, Rocco Gravino!"

"Hold on, girl, we're almost finished," Uncle Miltie cut her off. "Gravino, stay put! It's a hair off kilter. Tilt it a tad skyward."

"*Left?* You said *right!*" Rocky stumbled, barely keeping his footing.

Uncle Miltie waved his cane. "Enough! That's it."

Gracie took a deep breath. There was no sense reasoning with this pair. Rocky and Uncle Miltie (a.k.a. George Morgan) came from the same mold. Neither gave credence to common sense when it came to aging. Their stubborn natures defied actuarial tables. Why, Uncle Miltie was fond of declaring, he planned to wear out rather than rust out!

Gracie worried all the same, for her boys were not getting any younger. She and Rocky had started enjoying senior citizen benefits, while her darling uncle—well, he was ambling toward ninety.

His moving in with her after his wife died had made perfect sense, although at first, he seemed to depend on her more than she on him. But, before long, Uncle Miltie was her indispensable handyman and loving support.

Just as Gracie was about to protest once again, Rocky scrambled down the ladder with the agility of a man half his age. Gracie shook her head, refusing to allow his sly grin to sway her resolve. "Don't try the charm with me, Gravino. You could have gotten yourself killed!"

Rocky rolled his eyes at her concern, impatiently changing the subject. "When I got here, my sniffer detected minestrone and homemade bread."

She gave him an impressed look. "I baked four loaves this morning, and some zwieback toast for the Nickolson baby."

"I saw Terry at Hammie Miller's," Uncle Miltie told her, "strutting around as proud as a peacock. He was sporting a new pocketknife. A fancy, handmade piece. Said it cost him almost six hundred dollars."

"For a pocket knife!" Gracie was a little annoyed, thinking that the family might better have used the money elsewhere. Phyllis had kept her job at the hospital switchboard to help the household budget.

"Damascus steel," Rocky piped in. "It's a beaut. He showed it to me, too. Those knives are made out of fifty layers of top quality stainless steel. Terry's has a hand-carved handle, so it's going to be a collector's item."

Her uncle nodded. "Something to pass on to his son, at least so he says."

Gracie could only shake her head.

She closed her eyes a moment and asked the Lord to intercede. *Lord, I don't want to be judgmental. Guide me in heart and motive. Show me where I can be of some help to Phyllis and her family. And, please, watch over Katie, remind her of what is right. Lord, I don't want to believe she—or anyone else she knows—is taking what isn't theirs.*

"Tower to Gracie!" Rocky expected an answer to a question she hadn't heard. "So, when do we eat?"

"You think with your stomach, Gravino." Uncle Miltie gave a jab to his friend's middle. "And it looks like you have been thinking *too much*."

Rocky shot back a threat. "See here, my friend, you better watch what you're saying, or I might just climb right back up there and disconnect that new contraption of yours!"

"I'm going to fix supper." Gracie left them arguing. In the kitchen, Gooseberry hopped from the window sill to greet her.

"Watching the birds, I see." She bent to stroke her pumpkin-colored tabby. He purred loudly, rubbing against her legs.

"Jess told me she talked to you," Rocky said, walking and taking a deep breath. "Smells delicious."

Gracie smiled her appreciation at his appreciation, which she never seemed to tire of hearing. She handed him silverware to set the table. "I like her. I think you've made a good decision."

"I know she's trying to do a good job. Plus, they need her paycheck." He paused. "But I do worry about her, Gracie. She seems lonely, and often sad."

"I'm sure she feels overwhelmed at times, and that probably just drives her to work harder."

"When I tell her to knock off for the day," Rocky went on, "she always says yes and, the next time I look, she's still at her desk."

He hesitated, seeming to weigh his words. "Sometimes I

think she's avoiding going home. But she certainly seems to love her kids. Talks about them enough. Anyway, I think she could use a friend—someone to mother her a little."

"We've met only on a casual basis," Gracie told him, "but I sense we could be good friends." She couldn't resist. "She says you're quite the matchmaker!"

"I did a little networking. What's the harm in that?"

Gracie winked at him now. "Right!"

"*Networking*. That's all it was." He protested. She thrust the napkins at him.

"Well, it crossed *my* mind that Jess could be a good match for Paul. Call me old-fashioned, but I'd like to see our pastor married."

"So! I'm not the *only* amateur cupid around here!" Rocky grinned, and they laughed together.

"We're both romantics at heart."

"Speak for yourself. I was just being practical."

"Save your curmudgeon act for your staff—*we* both know you're an old softie. You'd like to see Paul and Jess get together."

"Paul's an okay guy—for a minister."

Gracie decided to let this statement go unchallenged.

"I respect your faith, Gracie," he went on. "And I respect Paul. He . . . seems . . . so . . . normal—"

"Normal?"

"A regular Joe."

She raised an eyebrow.

"A down-to-earth guy. He doesn't come across as squeaky-clean or holier-than-thou."

"You've been watching too many TV shows!" She looked at him. "And you know how they depict newspaper editors!"

She watched him grin ruefully. "Okay, you're right. And I know you think a little more exposure to Paul wouldn't hurt me, either."

She allowed her expression to convey her approval of his assumption. God would certainly handle Rocky Gravino in His good time. Always the pragmatist seeking Truth, her dear friend was destined for grace. Of that Gracie was sure.

"I just have a hard time buying into all that goes with religion."

"A good journalist would do some research," she reminded him. "He'd make his own evaluations, rather than relying on stereotypes."

"Point scored," he conceded.

She passed him the salad bowls. "You're a first-class news-paperman. Better yet, you're honest. Natural curiosity tempered with a good dose of pragmatism—what more could God ask for? A genuine seeker."

"Seek and you will find," Rocky replied. "I guess that's what you mean, on both the spiritual and temporal levels."

They grinned at one another with fond acceptance of their

differences. There were differences, Gracie thought, that God would one day render invisible.

"Anyway, thanks for befriending Jess," Rocky said, returning to their original subject. "It does sound like she's taken on a bit of a problem with this investment club. I told her that she should probably resign as treasurer, but she's afraid they'll think then that she might have had something to do with the missing funds."

Gracie sensed she was missing an important piece of information, one to which Rocky seemed privy. "But they had the deficit long before Jess joined their group."

"So she says."

"You think differently?"

"Doesn't matter what I think." He reached for the glasses Gracie handed him from the cupboard. "Often it doesn't matter what the facts really are. It only seems to matter what people believe the facts to be."

"I don't understand."

"Jess comes in and announces a discrepancy in the books. Yet no one in the group noticed it. The books could actually have been correctly balanced *before* she took over. Who is to say? Jess? They may wonder why she was so keen on being treasurer to begin with."

Gracie bristled. "You don't think she took the money?"

"I'm just trying to stay objective. Don't get me wrong,

Gracie, I like Jess. I don't want to believe she's taken it, but . . ."

Rocky paused, choosing his words carefully.

"But what?" Gracie hugged the glass pitcher she'd retrieved from the cupboard. She did not like the implication, not one little bit. "I believe her," she said firmly. "Don't you?"

"Of course I do." Rocky was adamant. "The question is: Does the group?"

Gracie filled the pitcher with ice, then reached to the counter for the pot of steeped tea. "They *have* to believe her. It's easy enough to check. She's only been doing the books a month."

Rocky held out his glass for her to fill. "Exactly. And she's the only one to have noticed that the money is missing."

"Jess organized the records and calculated their deposits. Surely, they can't argue with bank receipts."

"As I understand it, the problem is not with the bank receipts, but with the stock portfolio. At first, she assumed it involved an adjustment for market value of the stocks. Now, she's not so sure. Following the investment trail is going to be tough, considering the club's casualness about bookkeeping."

Gracie was not convinced that the entire club might doubt the integrity of their newest member. "Money can always be tracked."

"You're right, but not always easily or simply."

Rocky took a gulp of tea, and eyed her as if unsure of how

much more to confide. "Besides, Jess does have another reason for concern." He seemed reluctant to say more.

Gracie's worried expression was probably impossible for him to ignore. Especially if he wanted dinner on time. "All I know is that her husband was the protegé of some important scientist, and that Jess kept their lab's account books.

"Jess hired an independent auditor to do the books after her husband's death. Some slight discrepancies turned up. When she told me that, I offered to check into it on her behalf. There had been some serious venture capital money involved—Jess's husband and his mentor, Dr. Carroll Samuels, were on the track of some valuable patents. It wasn't just science, it was business. Big business, potentially."

Gracie was trying to put it all together in her mind. "Oh, my."

"Plus, it doesn't help that she's virtually broke."

Her eyes widened. "Broke? Well, she did say her nest egg was meager and the insurance money would go for the children's education."

"It turned out she had to settle some very large debts her husband had that she wasn't aware of. Everything she received has gone to take care of those, and, in the process, she's inherited a poor credit rating, along with a bit of a blot on her own bookkeeping abilities."

"Oh, my," Gracie said again.

"Marilyn Clayton is her neighbor and reached out to her,

to join the club. Jess hadn't had any intimate friendships since before her husband got sick. Then she moved here. She'd been busy with her kids. And with being a part of his work."

Gracie understood. Her own healing had come through the support of her fellow choir members at Eternal Hope Community Church, and through the steady love offered her by her friends and neighbors.

Rocky must have been reading her mind. "I know you're dying to get her involved in that church of yours. And, frankly, Gracie, I think it would be a great idea. Maybe she could tap into that direct line to the Almighty you all seem to enjoy. Lord knows, she could use His help."

"We all have a direct line to God," she reminded him.

"Okay, I'll give you that, but some of you seem to be on the special frequent-caller plan, one Jess could benefit from."

"So, what else can I do to help?" Gracie asked. "I told her that I would talk to Phyllis Nickolson, get a feel for what she knows. I'm going to find a way to approach Darla Knight. Marilyn Clayton and I are old friends, so I'm going to check in with her, as well. Marybeth Bower's in the choir with me." Gracie poured tea in the glasses. "Now I understand why Jess is reluctant to confront the group. I thought she seemed overly distraught for a discrepancy that developed before she took over as treasurer. But, I mean, really, the facts should take care of themselves.

"I think Jess is really a proud person. Very independent. And she's a newcomer here. You can't blame her for being a little apprehensive about being accepted into such a tight community."

Rocky flashed her a grin. "I still wonder if *I've* been accepted."

"You could put out a better newspaper," Gracie teased. "At least according to Cordelia Fountain, who always wants more coverage from you for the tourist home and its architectural heritage."

"I'm not sure how much of this I should have told you," Rocky said, after a moment's reflection. His tone had turned cautious. "Let's keep this between the two of us, okay? Jess's history is her own business."

"Mum's the word."

He seemed genuinely relieved.

"I can see you care about Jess. She's lucky to have you for an employer," Gracie told him. "I know she admires you greatly. You're such an old softie."

"So you say. But I'm a tough employer. Jess applied for the job, and we clicked. That's all that matters. Until proven otherwise, she has my full confidence and I'll back her when it comes to any of these situations."

Gracie shook her head. "You're not a softie, you're pure marshmallow."

Rocky laughed. "Seriously now, Gracie. I like her and can

see how tough she's had it. She even apologized for the gap in her employment, as though raising those two great little kids wasn't experience enough."

Gracie recalled her years of being a stay-at-home mother. Now, things were different. There were more choices, most of them difficult. It seemed to her her daughter-in-law had struck a nice balance: Wendy worked part-time, and her dance studio was located in the same building. She thanked God that Arlen and Wendy had found a workable model. Now she would ask the Lord to guide this other young mother in her quest for the right path.

"What can we do to help her?"

"Me? I don't know." He flashed a grin. "*You*, I suppose, have already set to praying."

"All's well," Gracie assured him. "You know me."

He eyed her fondly.

Gracie continued, "I'm going to keep on praying that Jess trusts me enough to tell the whole story. I do want to help her, but I need all the facts."

"I told her that you were a straight shooter—a kind of angel in an apron, a saint in sneakers, a real handmaiden to a higher power."

"Okay, okay!" Gracie held up her hands. "You've made your point. Let's eat!"

UNCLE MILTIE AMBLED into the kitchen just as Rocky had finished setting the table. He stared at them, sensing an area of possible interest being discussed. Her darling uncle hated to miss out on anything, but Gracie felt that Jess Horton's life was off-limits for the time being. Rocky had trusted her with his confidences.

"Hammie Miller wants me to run an Old Timers' column," Rocky said, changing the subject. "Maybe even a whole page with vintage ads and nostalgia. Seems *everybody* is an editor."

Rocky looked at Uncle Miltie. "Hammie thinks I should solicit contributions from his regulars. He says it might even boost circulation."

"How's that?" Her uncle seemed genuinely curious.

"You guys may then actually *buy* my papers once in a while, just to see your name in print, instead of borrowing his copy."

Her uncle let loose with a belly laugh. "You know I read the *Gazette* here at home! But I take your point, even if the others might resist seeing it! Between saving a quarter or seeing their names in print—it's still going to be a tough call!"

Miller's Feed Store was an old-fashioned agricultural supply emporium, right down to the plank flooring and blue enamel pot perking Hammie's famous coffee. The business had been in the family for generations. Young Hammie had embraced the legacy, encouraging the local male population to drop in.

But an Old Timers' feature! There wasn't anyone she knew fonder of reminiscing than George Morgan. He was a tireless spinner of historical trivia, boyhood episodes, harrowing war tales and, of course, his bad jokes.

"The paper could give me a special box!" Uncle Miltie was enthusiastic. "You could call it 'Good Medicine.'"

"'Good Medicine'?" Rocky flashed him a skeptical look.

"Why sure, laughter is the *best* medicine." Uncle Miltie looked at Gracie. "And not everyone thinks my jokes aren't funny."

"They're cornier than a tamale factory!" she pronounced.

He chuckled. "Funny runs in the family, wouldn't you say? Maybe, instead of Uncle Miltie, you'd rather call me Pop Corn?"

"I'd rather call you quiet, but I'd be pretty close to breaking a Commandment!"

Rocky shook his head. "You two!"

"You serious about this?" Uncle Miltie returned to the subject.

"I don't know," Rocky conceded. "We're looking for ways to find new readers. Or win back former ones. A vintage page might be just the ticket, and not just for older folks. I think younger ones might be intrigued, too. Hammie talked about sponsoring the page, and I like the idea of running old photographs and memorabilia from our archives."

"And jokes! Don't forget the jokes." Her uncle was being serious in the matter of humor.

Long ago he had been nicknamed "Uncle Miltie" after Milton Berle, the legendary television comedian. Now he was practically a legend in his own time, or at least in his own adopted hometown. Secretly, Gracie, as she listened, hoped Rocky would honor his request. "You have to admit," she laughed, "his jokes are *vintage*."

"The problem is, we have a lot on our plate right now, what with the new weekend edition and starting up a religion page. I've got one editor on that, and she's all I can spare right now. I also have our regular features to consider, and the advertising." He reminded them, "This isn't Chicago. We have a tight budget."

"But you said yourself that Hammie is willing to sponsor it," Gracie reminded him.

"Unfortunately, it isn't all smooth sailing right now. I'm

not even sure if that new page will begin as scheduled. We may have to put it off until next month."

"How's that?" Uncle Miltie wanted to know.

Rocky dodged the question, since Jess Horton's involvement was what made for a possible delay.

"I just don't want to have too many irons in the fire," he answered simply. And to Gracie he said, "I thought you claimed dinner was ready."

She took the hint. "You boys go wash up." No more talk of Jess tonight, she understood.

"Boys?" Uncle Miltie hooked his thumbs under his suspenders. "You see any boys here, you can just send them home to their mamas."

Gracie laughed, but Rocky said wistfully, "I'd give anything to do just that." Then he turned to Uncle Miltie and asked in all seriousness, "Wouldn't you like to go home again? I mean, *really*. Wouldn't it be great to have supper as a boy again—just one more time?"

Uncle Miltie joined Rocky at the sink and, grabbing the towel, seemed lost in his own thoughts. Memories were gifts, Gracie decided. They were best unwrapped slowly.

She sighed, recalling her own mother's sparkling blue eyes. Although shadowed as she grew older by the pain of arthritis, those eyes were always eager to watch over Gracie. She would tenderly keep her mother alive in her heart,

Gracie knew, and like her boys, she would, just once, love to go home for dinner again.

"My mother was one tough Italian lady," Rocky said after a while. "She was not only the best cook in our neighborhood, but she could get a straight story from the shiftiest of my friends. You came clean with Mama Gravino, no matter what. That laser-sharp gaze of hers looked straight into your heart."

Uncle Miltie nodded, adding some reminiscences of his own. "My mother was the same. Might as well fess up and face the music with her. She could get to the truth quicker than my brother and I could come up with an excuse."

"Let that be a lesson to you both," Gracie teased. "There's something to be said for women's intuition."

"That's 'sleuth sense' with you, my dear," Rocky corrected. "I told Jess Horton as much. If there's anybody who can help her solve the mystery of the missing money, it's you, Gracie Lynn Parks."

Uncle Miltie stopped in the middle of pulling out Gracie's chair. "Missing money?"

Gooseberry hopped down from his perch on the windowsill, as if to say, "The cat is out of the bag."

Uncle Miltie demanded, "What money?"

"It's probably a bookkeeping error," Gracie said, providing just enough information to satisfy her uncle, or so she hoped.

"An editor of mine is a member of a local ladies' investment group," Rocky added.

"That's got to be the Kidnappers," Uncle Miltie said.

"How do *you* know about them?" Gracie demanded. The sly old jokester didn't miss a trick, keeping his fingers on the pulse of the community. Obviously, the *Gazette* wasn't the only news that circulated around the feed store.

"The members did a presentation at the library a few months back." Uncle Miltie pulled out his seat. "I was there for my story hour with the kids, and figured I'd just stay and maybe learn a few things about investing the money I don't have."

He smiled broadly.

"Nice group of ladies. You say they're missing some money?"

"I don't actually know," she admitted.

"Their treasurer has reason to question the bookkeeping," Rocky said, and now gave him a thumbnail description of the problem.

Uncle Miltie whistled. "I'd say there's been a thief in the cookie jar, alright."

"That's what Jess thinks," Rocky told him.

"She's the editor you've assigned to the new religion page," Uncle Miltie said. "Jess is the treasurer in question?"

Gracie looked at Rocky, who gave a helpless shrug. There

was no use trying to keep secrets from Uncle Miltie. Gooseberry meowed agreement.

"I don't how much I can tell you," Rocky said. "It'd be one thing if I were truly involved, myself, but I'm not."

"My lips are zipped," Uncle Miltie said, making the appropriate gesture to accompany his vow.

Gracie, in their defense, reminded Rocky how cooperatively the three of them had worked in the past. They were a team. Besides, she was fairly certain Jess wouldn't mind Uncle Miltie understanding the situation. If the cat had escaped the bag, so be it. She smiled encouragingly.

So Rocky went over the basics of the tale, and, hearing it again, Gracie was increasingly doubtful that there'd been a simple miscalculation in bookkeeping. The more she heard, the more convinced she became that Jess was right: someone in the group *had* taken that money.

"The problem is, most of these women go to church together," Rocky concluded. "And Jess is the newcomer. They don't want to believe one of their own is stealing from the others."

"We can't fault them for that," Uncle Miltie said. "No more than the Disciples wanted to acknowledge the betrayer in their midst."

He looked at Gracie. "You think there's a Judas here?"

She shuddered.

"Maybe you can figure out who's the guilty party," Rocky proposed. "You've a way of getting at the heart of the matter, my dear. And I did have the wisdom to send Jess to talk to you."

Gracie didn't reply. She had already begun to consider the problems facing Jess Horton her own. But her next step was still unknown to her. "Supper is getting cold. Uncle Miltie, would you say grace?"

"Lord, we thank You for Your generosity, especially for this scrumptious meal, and for the beautiful cook who provided it." He squeezed her hand. "Bless our fellowship around this table, and may everything said be honoring You."

Rocky's "Amen" was almost as enthusiastic as his request for her homemade corn muffins.

Uncle Miltie polished off one butter-drenched muffin before starting on the soup.

"So, Gracie," Rocky said, continuing. "It looks like you've got another mystery on your hands."

Uncle Miltie balanced his spoon in mid-air. "It was an inside job, I suppose."

"Looks that way." Rocky said. "A lot of them Gracie knows from church. Those 'Kidnappers,' I mean."

Gracie smiled at him. "Pastor Paul is fond of saying that church is not a hotel for saints, but a hospital for sinners."

Rocky grinned back. The three friends ate on in companionable silence for a few moments.

After a while, Uncle Miltie said, frowning, "You know, I never can get used to the idea of eating stuff that's afraid to come out in the sunshine." He held out a mushroom on his spoon.

"Sometimes, I can tell you," Rocky said slyly, "I feel like one."

"A mushroom?" Gracie raised an eyebrow.

"Well, my staff likes to keep me in the dark!"

"So, that means you'll like this one," Uncle Miltie said, smoothly seizing the opening.

"A mushroom walked into a ballroom and saw a very pretty girl, so he asked her to dance. 'I never dance with mushrooms,' she told him. 'Well why not?' the mushroom asked. 'Just ask anyone—I'm a *fun* guy!'"

The only sound was the clink of silverware.

"So, how about that section we were discussing? 'Good Medicine.'" Her uncle fixed a stern eye on Rocky. "Come on, what do you say?"

"Let me get this religion page up and running first. If I still have an editor, that is."

Gracie shut her eyes and prayed.

5

GRACIE TOOK A SEAT at the Nickolsons' kitchen counter, next to the baby. Darren Michael sat in his high chair playing with the zwieback she'd baked and brought over for him. He waved the gummy toast, chattering to no one in particular.

Gracie remembered Arlen as a baby. He had loved zwieback. And his son Elmo almost as much. Her grandson had a cowlick in the same place. Gracie missed them both terribly.

She sighed. "They don't stay babies for long."

"No they don't," Phyllis said, positioning herself on the other side of Darren.

"Enjoy him while you can." Gracie made a mental note to call Arlen that evening. Listening to Elmo's chatter would help satisfy the small ache she felt all the time at being such a distance from them.

Phyllis said, "I do try to savor every moment. It's hard

though. We get so busy. I know I missed a lot with Katie. After my husband left, I had to work full-time. She got short-changed."

Phyllis rested her chin on her knuckles. "If only I had a magic wand! I'd love to have it to do over again—and spend more time with Katie."

Yes, time was so important. And there was never enough of it. Gracie would have made better use of it with Arlen. Sure, she'd carved out big chunks of her day to take him to the park, play games on the family room floor and teach him to bake cookies. But there were also many moments she had somehow let pass by. There always were.

"No use fretting over the past," she reasoned out loud. "God's given us today to enjoy. And tomorrow."

She and Arlen had plenty of wonderful memories. And now she had a delightful grandson, one with whom she planned to spend lots of time despite the distance between them. After all, New York was just a couple of hours away by plane. *That's all I ask, Lord. Keep them in Your tender care.*

"You're right," Phyllis said. "God's gifts are many, and each day is precious in itself." She leaned over to kiss her son.

"Is he walking yet?" Gracie asked, enjoying the special moment between mother and son.

"He pulls himself up on the furniture. Loves to have Katie walk him around the house."

"I always wanted a little brother or sister for Arlen." Gracie was surprised by her confession. "But he says he's happy as an only child. He and Wendy plan to have only one."

"You'll just have to spoil him royally," Phyllis told her. "My mom says that. She loves to spoil Katie. And now Darren. Two are double the fun, she says."

"My mother had a rhyme," Gracie remembered. "Something about cobwebs waiting and dust going to sleep, because she was rocking the baby and babies don't keep."

"That's cute," Phyllis sighed. "My mom now lives in Illinois. It's only a five-hour drive away, but with a baby, that can feel like an eternity. The result is we don't see her often enough."

Gracie nodded. "I don't visit with my son and his family enough, either."

"I sympathize with the position your son and daughter-in-law are in," Phyllis said. "I wish my mother was here to babysit like she did when Katie was little. They had a special relationship."

Sadness tugged at Gracie's heart. She did miss that opportunity.

"Katie gets along wonderfully with my father," Phyllis went on. "If only they could spend more time together."

Gracie sought the woman's gaze. "Are things better with Terry and Katie?"

"Well, it isn't getting worse is all I can say. He tries—but now, with Darren, she's just so jealous."

Gracie nodded sympathetically.

"The slightest extra attention to him throws her into a tizzy."

"She's really just a child herself," Gracie reminded her.

"That's easy to forget, I'm afraid, probably because then I start feeling guilty."

Gracie reached for her friend's hand.

"Thanks for listening," Phyllis squeezed back.

Darren squealed happily, tossing his toast to the dog that now appeared in the doorway. The cocker spaniel sniffed and turned up his nose at the toast before settling himself at the foot of the high chair.

Phyllis pushed her chair out to retrieve Darren's teething toast and throw it in the garbage. She wiped his face and scooped him out of the high chair.

"I saw Katie at the mall," Gracie ventured to say.

"She spends way too much time there." Phyllis put her little boy on the floor next to her, and watched as he pulled himself to stand. "She comes home all the more dissatisfied every time she goes."

"Why do you let her go?" Gracie wondered.

"It's hard to say no," Phyllis answered matter-of-factly. "All her friends go."

"Things were easier when I was raising children," Gracie admitted. "We didn't have malls, so kids made do with back-yard tree forts and endless games of sidewalk four-square."

Phyllis kept her focus on her toddler. "Gracie, Katie seems to be moving in a fast lane I don't really recognize. Her friends are older and much more worldly. I don't like it, but I don't know what to do. Things have been so difficult here at home, her going out like this has meant some blessed peace."

Phyllis kept her attention on Darren. She looked at Gracie. "Katie didn't mention that she saw you at the mall—but then she doesn't tell me much of anything any more."

"I thought things were better between you now," Gracie said.

"For a while, she seemed genuinely interested in helping with the baby. She'd even sometimes join Terry and me in a game of Scrabble in the evening."

Phyllis explained that Katie and Ashley Knight had been friends almost since the sandbox. But the girls had grown apart in middle school—according to Phyllis—because Ashley was set on becoming part of the popular group.

"Katie is shy, and we definitely don't have the money to keep up with the Joneses. Most months, we can barely make ends meet on my part-time salary at the hospital and what Terry brings home."

She looked at Gracie. "Frankly, I'm surprised that Ashley

has made friends with Katie again. There's no social clout to be gained."

Did Gracie detect a tinge of bitterness?

"Katie seems to think we're made of money, no matter what I say. Why, just the other week she begged us for a sweater that cost eighty dollars."

Phyllis described the influence of Ashley's extravagant shopping habits. "The girl wears an outfit once and discards it, often tossing things to Katie or the other girls like scraps. It's embarrassing, Gracie. I've told Darla as much, but she doesn't seem to understand."

Gracie just listened.

"Terry was upset at first, too. But he could see Katie was getting defensive—angry, even—so, for the sake of an evening's peace, we decided to drop it. We can't afford to buy those brand names, so what did it hurt, really, if Ashley was giving them to Katie?"

Phyllis paused, apparently reexamining the wisdom of that decision. "Ashley is always giving Katie things, not just clothing, but jewelry and CDs. I don't know where she gets the money."

"Darla's a single mom, isn't she?" Gracie decided to press the issue. "I didn't realize that she was so well-off."

"Her ex is pretty generous—owns a mail-order warehouse. I think he sells office supplies. And Darla recently got her real-estate license. I know she's made a few sales because she's purchased some stocks on her own."

Phyllis paused again, thinking. "Ashley used to boast she had her dad wrapped around her little finger. But then he remarried. And his new wife has two young children. Things just might change."

Gracie's heart went out to any children dealing with such heartaches. *Lord, strengthen our families.*

"Where is Katie now?" she asked.

Phyllis hesitated once again. "My husband rarely considers the impact of his actions." She turned her attention to Darren, lifting him to her lap. "Terry bought an expensive pocket knife, bragging it would be an heirloom for his *only* child." Phyllis's eyes welled with tears. "Katie didn't handle it very well."

Gracie reached out to touch her again. "What happened?"

"She blew up at Terry and ran out of the house, screaming that she was never coming back. Terry told her, 'good riddance.'" Phyllis was crying now. "He didn't mean it. Darla called to tell me that Katie was over at her place."

She sniffed, pulling herself together, as Darren looked up wide-eyed. "Darla offered to keep Katie for the weekend. I don't how much she told them. They headed to some outlet mall a couple of hours drive from here. I was embarrassed, Gracie, but what could I say?"

Gracie didn't know.

"It will do Katie and Terry good to have some cool-down

time," Phyllis said, obviously trying to convince herself.

"Would you like me to take Darren for a walk?" Gracie asked, hoping to be of some help to this frazzled mother.

"No, I'm going to give him a bath and feed him. I've been trying to get him to take one long nap in the afternoon." She smiled. "Anyway, you've given me the best gift with your presence. I miss my mom. Having you here today is a godsend."

"I only wish that I could be more help." Gracie stood to leave. "If there's anything I can do. . . ."

The telephone rang, and Phyllis excused herself, motioning Gracie to wait. Gracie stood in the modest living room. A port-a-crib sat in the corner, and Katie's school desk was in another. It looked to be close quarters for a family of four, something she'd never really thought about before.

As Phyllis talked on the phone with Terry, Gracie lifted the family to the Lord. *Oh, Lord, take Katie under Your wing, guide her and provide her with strong friends to help her be strong.*

When she opened her eyes, Phyllis stood in front of her. "You said on the phone before you came over that there was something you wanted to talk to me about. I know it wasn't Katie."

Gracie bent to pick up Darren, who was making his way around the chairs at the table. "He certainly is a cutie!"

"A little imp!" Phyllis cooed to her baby, now in Gracie's arms. "So, what is it you wanted to talk to me about?"

Gracie was glad she had Darren as a distraction, to help her with her discomfort at broaching such a touchy subject. "Jess Horton was talking to me about your investment group, the Kidnappers—such a cute name, I always thought—since Marge and I have been thinking of starting one."

Phyllis studied her for a moment. "Did she mention the deficit?"

That comment caught Gracie by surprise.

"Darla told me—in confidence," Phyllis told her. "I certainly hope it turns out to be a bookkeeping error. We'd hate to think our newest member is dishonest."

"You think Jess took it?"

"I don't want to think anyone *took* it," Phyllis stumbled over her words. "Darla says it's probably a mistake. She's going to get her accountant to look at the books." Phyllis took Darren back. "None of us have had any reason to check the books. We just assumed we had what was listed on the ledger."

Gracie tried to get everything straight in her mind. "So as far as the group was concerned, the books balanced? Who was treasurer before Jess?"

"I was in charge of recording our dues and mailing the checks to the broker." Phyllis's gaze narrowed.

"I'm not doubting you, just trying to understand how things worked with the group."

Phyllis nodded. "The problem is in our stock portfolio."

"And who kept track of that?"

A nervous chuckle. "I know it seems crazy for an investment group, but none of us likes bookkeeping, so we just let it take care of itself. We never really audited our portfolio. It simply accumulated. We don't even have a flesh-and-blood broker anymore—didn't need one, since we'd switched to an online company. Pretty stupid for an investment club, you'd think."

She looked at Gracie. "We're all friends. We started as young mothers, looking for something to do when we all got together. Making money was a lark. I really don't want to think someone took it."

Gracie thought she noticed a slight change of color in Phyllis's staid gray eyes. Perhaps Darla and Phyllis *did* suspect Jess of fabricating a deficit to shift the blame and cover herself.

Phyllis rubbed Darren's back, and the baby snuggled closer. "I better give him his bath, or he's going to fall back to sleep."

"I know you're in a difficult position," Gracie told her. "You're all friends. I'm just glad to hear you're remaining optimistic. Let's pray this is merely an oversight."

"I like Jess."

"So do I," Gracie confessed. "And I know she appreciates your friendship."

"Single parenting isn't easy—I know, all too well. My heart

goes out to her, Gracie, really it does. I'm so thankful for Terry. Really I am. He's good with the baby, so when he comes home in the afternoon, I can work a couple of hours." Phyllis kissed her son's head. "It works out nicely. Terry is here to play with him after his nap, while he fixes supper. Katie does homework. I usually get home about seven and after we eat, Terry has time to mess around on the computer. Poor Jess has got to do it alone."

Darren began to squirm. "I'll try to call her more often— make an effort to get together."

"Are you ready for your bath?" Gracie asked Darren. "That will be great fun!"

"He loves to play in the water. These days, we're both drenched by the time he's finished." Phyllis swung her son up to nuzzle his face.

"I'll let myself out," Gracie said. "You've got your hands full, literally!"

Phyllis's expression turned serious. "Gracie, don't worry. Nobody knows but Darla and me, and we're not blaming Jess. We're still hoping there was a mistake in the accounting."

Gracie was praying for that, as well.

"We've been an informal group all along, more interested in learning the ropes than balancing the books. None of us are number-crunchers. We were all thrilled when Jess offered to take over as treasurer, but now . . ."

"You said you didn't doubt her honesty."

"I don't. Darla doesn't want to suspect her, either. It's just that everything was fine until she joined the group."

"You've all been together since the beginning?" Gracie asked as they walked to door. "All five of you?"

Phyllis shook her head. "Four since the beginning—Betsey Griswold, Marilyn Clayton, Marybeth Bower and myself. Two of the original members moved. Darla joined us two years ago. And now, we've added Jess Horton."

"Why Jess?"

"Marilyn Clayton suggested it—they're neighbors."

Marybeth Bower, one of Eternal Hope's altos, was married to the police chief, and she couldn't cheat anyone if she tried. Marilyn Clayton had her hands full with Patsy. The poor child had been crippled from birth. Although she didn't know Marilyn—who had a second daughter, Laura—very well, she'd known her long enough to judge her a woman whose commitment to her family and community was beyond question.

The Griswolds were Gracie's neighbors. Betsey made her children apologize for picking Gracie's lilacs without asking, so, of course, she didn't fit the profile of an embezzler.

Then there was Darla Knight. Gracie didn't know as much about her. But a real-estate agent with a wealthy ex-husband didn't seem a likely suspect.

It couldn't possibly be Phyllis. Could it? She glanced back at the careworn woman standing on her front steps, holding her baby. Darren was pulling at his mother's hair and kicking happily as Gracie waved a final good-bye.

If Phyllis had any secrets, she was doing an impressive job of hiding them.

"Bye, Gracie!" she called as she turned and went inside.

P ASTOR PAUL WAS CHANGING the announcements on the church bulletin board when Gracie arrived for choir practice. "Doesn't Pat usually do that?" she asked, realizing suddenly she hadn't seen the church secretary in over a week. Silently, Gracie prayed nothing was wrong.

"Pat took a few days off, since her mother is having surgery." Paul finished pinning up the last announcement. "How about putting Vera and Pat on the prayer chain? The operation's in a few days."

Vera Crossley was a capable eighty-seven years old, and had recently moved back to Willow Bend to live in an efficiency apartment for seniors. Luckily, Pat's sister, Emily Wicks, also was nearby and could be with their mother when she returned from the hospital.

Gracie made a mental note to call Pat about visiting her mother after the surgery. She had a new strudel recipe she was eager to try, and Vera seemed the perfect recipient.

"Rode by your house the other day, and I see you got yourself a satellite dish," Paul said.

Gracie rolled her eyes. "Uncle Miltie got *himself* one."

"I hope he gets those all-comedy channels. He could use a few new jokes!" Paul laughed. "I'm a big soccer fan, so I'm hoping you'll invite me over once in a while. I don't have cable."

Gracie was tempted to remind her pastor that he didn't even have a television. Why, when his mother and father came for an extended visit, they had to buy extra kitchen utensils.

"I know what you're thinking."

She smiled. "How could you?"

"I can read you like my mom. I'll have you know I did buy a TV. I got a good deal at the thrift store. And it works, too!"

She shook her head. "You need a woman in your life."

"I need a better paying job!" He laughed. "No, seriously, objects don't matter much to me. I guess that's a side effect of having served in a third-world country."

His smile was endearing. "Think you can find me a woman who enjoys shopping the secondhand stores? She's got to like pizza, Chinese food and canned soup, or be an awful good cook herself."

"I might know such a person." Gracie was enjoying the conversation. "Just met her the other day."

"I think I know who you mean."

Did Gracie detect an interested gleam in her pastor's blue eyes? She would let *him* tell *her* about the pretty young editor at the *Mason County Gazette*.

And he did, saying Jess Horton had already contacted him about his becoming a contributor to the Saturday edition. "We got to chatting, and she mentioned that she'd met you."

He picked out a couple of push pins. Gracie waited to see if she could detect any hint of special interest in Jess.

"Rocky's experimenting with a religion page," he told her, knowing full well that she knew. "I'm kind of excited."

"About the religion page?" She swallowed a chuckle.

He was clearly embarrassed. "Of course—what did you think?"

She grinned as he fumbled over his words.

"I thought I would polish some of the pieces I did for our church newsletter. You know the ones, 'Notes from the Pastor's Desk.'"

"They're wonderful, but. . ." Gracie paused. She tried to work out a tactful way to address the suggestion. Paul's columns tended to meander, so his pastoral writings might be a trifle too, well, parochial, for a newspaper looking to broaden its appeal.

"You've a got a knack for bringing lessons to life with your examples," she said, truthfully. "Uncle Miltie loves your parables, and so do I. They're down to earth and easy to understand. I know that they'd be encouraging even to the least churched of our community."

"You think I should dig out some old sermons?"

She met his gaze. "For ideas. Folks don't expect to read a sermon in a newspaper. To hold their interest, you need to keep it short."

"Jess *did* say her boss is tough." He chuckled. "I told her that Rocky, as we here in the community know, subscribes to the KISS method of journalism."

"I'm almost afraid to ask what it stands for."

"Keep It Simple, Stupid." Paul chuckled again.

She shook her head, imagining Rocky growling out that maxim to his staff.

"And that's probably good advice for the clergy, as well," Paul said ruefully. "I've noticed more than a few bobbing heads during my sermons."

She patted his shoulder. "We all love you, Paul."

"But?"

"You must keep in mind that some of us in the congregation are age-impaired," she warned him. "We're prone to mid-morning drowsiness."

He laughed.

"You do a wonderful job. Everyone says so. You're a first-class preacher."

"Who needs a wife."

"You can read my mind."

"Years of practice with Mom." His expression turned bashful. "Now, don't be writing my mother, but Jess and I have made a plan to get together—"

"For a date?"

"Not a date, no, definitely not a date."

"So, what is it?"

"We're meeting at Celestial City. To talk about the column over eggroll. It's just a meeting, that's all."

Paul raked his hands through his unruly blond hair. "I offered to pick her up, but she didn't think it a good idea, saying it might confuse or upset her children."

"She's looking out for their welfare," Gracie assured him.

"Of course, I understand."

He met her gaze. "I'm really not very good at this— I get all tongue-tied."

She did feel sorry for the man, and guilty for enjoying his discomfort. "But this isn't a date."

"No, no, it is definitely *not* a date." He glanced around. "Please don't mention it to anyone else. The ladies of our congregation have been anything but discreet about hoping to see me married."

Gracie feigned surprise. "Really? I guess it's normal."

"You're right, and so the hints are anything but subtle," he told her. "Why, just yesterday, Marge pitched the new guidance counselor at the high school. She's single, I'm told, and she's sensible."

The women of the church had done their share of optimistic mismatching when it came to their own available and attractive bachelor. And her friend Marge Lawrence was the main instigator.

"Speaking of matchmaking!" Gracie looked up as Marge stood before them.

"Fill me in," Marge demanded. "I've arrived at just the right moment, I see."

Paul beamed at her. "I was discussing with Gracie the hopes and dreams of the single clergy."

"And here I thought you'd found someone for *me*," Marge joked.

Marge, in fact, hardly had time for serious husband-hunting, what with her successful gift shop and helping Gracie out with her catering jobs. Not to mention the Eternal Hope choir.

"So, what's the scoop?" Marge scanned the bulletin board. "I see your parents are looking for donations to their new mission in eastern Europe. I can never be sure of their whereabouts—I just know they follow their hearts around the world, doing the Lord's work.

She pointed next to the announcement Paul had just pinned to the board. "You're finally going to launch that Brown-Bag Bible Study. Count me in. And you, Gracie?"

Gracie barely had a chance to nod when Paul reminded Marge that the class met at noon, when she'd be at the shop.

"That's the pleasure of owning your own business," Marge reminded him. "I can close for lunch."

She turned toward Gracie. "Besides, now Marilyn Clayton's working for me part-time. Did you realize how well that investment club of hers is doing?" She explained to Paul, "Gracie and I have been talking about starting our own."

"I should talk to her," Paul said. "My folks are always dogging me to plan for my retirement. An investment club might be just the ticket."

"Gals only!" Marge told him. "It's all the rage, you know—female investment groups. You fellows are just too competitive."

Paul started to say something, but Marge said hastily, "No offense intended, truly. It's a girl thing, you know—we prefer less work and more socializing."

Turning to Gracie, she said, "Marilyn invited us to their next meeting. They're going to have someone specializing in long-term care insurance."

"Long-term care insurance?" Paul waited to hear more.

"Protection in the event that you need assisted living arrangements, or nursing care. Those services can rather quickly deplete a life savings."

"You're right," he told her. "John and Mazie Carothers never anticipated the skyrocketing cost of care or how long they'd be forced to rely on it."

Gracie knew he had a point. The last time she'd visited the couple, they'd expressed concern about the cost of their private nursing home.

"They now meet on Mondays at seven-thirty," Marge said. "We'll go together."

"Jess Horton belongs to an investment group," Paul offered. "She intimated discreetly they have some touchy financial issues to clear up."

"It's the same group," Gracie confirmed. "Everybody is hoping it's a bookkeeping error, but Jess wanted me to look into the situation."

Paul nodded. "She *did* seem quite concerned, although she didn't share the particulars. Only that she had problems."

It appeared that now more than a few people knew about Jess's problems. Could the woman be garnering sympathy to cover herself? No, Jess just did not seem disingenuous. Gracie felt sure she was honest to the bone, and she regarded herself as a keen judge of character.

"Jess is a widow with two young children," Paul was telling Marge. "Her family's nowhere near here, so she'd probably appreciate a little mothering." He winked at Gracie. "And *grand*mothering. Her kids are her pride and joy, just as Elmo is yours."

It warmed Gracie that her pastor recognized what yearnings in her were incompletely satisfied. Although she enjoyed a wonderful relationship with little Elmo, her grandson, they never seemed to have enough time together. How she longed to spoil him on a more regular basis!

"I sympathize with Jess's mother's position, being so far away." Gracie told them. "I can certainly try to be a surrogate grandma."

At the same time she shook off an unbecoming twinge of jealousy, as she imagined some older woman at Arlen's church "adopting" her little Elmo. Children needed all the love they could get, after all. And love seemed to come most generously packaged in grandparents.

"I don't think I know her," Marge said. "Which service does the family attend?"

"They don't have a church yet," Paul confided, with a conspiratorial smile. "But we're going to change that, aren't we?"

"Well, she's holding back for now," Gracie pointed out. "Our friendship may be just the encouragement she needs to settle into a church family."

"She's new to town," Paul told Marge. "Settled in Willow Bend after her husband's death. Rocky gave her a job at the *Gazette*."

"And that's why she wants me to look into the problem with the investment club," Gracie explained. "She just joined, and is understandably cautious of ruffling feathers."

Paul nodded. "I sense she's afraid of jeopardizing the new

friendships she's just made. She doesn't know us well enough to realize how tight this *Tie* binds."

"Amen!" Marge grinned as she caught the reference to the hymn they sang each Sunday.

"I'd been hoping to snag an invitation to visit the investment group," Gracie said. "It looks like you've done it for us, Marge."

Her friend chuckled. "You and me, Gracie Lynn Parks, are going to turn in our aprons and find out how to become stockbrokers! Or, as Uncle Miltie might say, we'll take stock and go for broke! And, even better, there's a mystery on the side."

"I'm glad you're involved, and are going to a meeting, Gracie," Paul told her. "You'll have Jess's problem, and the club's, solved before those children even wake up!"

"They're a long way past needing naps," Marge reminded them. "Most of them are in your youth group now."

As Paul said he'd only been teasing—he knew the origins of the group and found the name charming—Gracie remembered her encounter with Jim Thompson at the mall. She prayed with all her heart that certain of those once-napping kids weren't also shoplifters. And that none of their mothers were breaking rules, either.

Lord, I send up my deepest, dearest wish that I find no wrongdoers. I'll be happy to unearth misperceptions or honest errors, and I know You'll guide me to the truth, whatever it may be.

Paul now crossed his arms and leaned against the bulletin board. "It seems money is a universal provider for most anything but happiness."

"And a passport to everywhere but eternity," Marge added.

"No wonder the Lord preached on it more than any other subject," Paul said.

Marge laughed. "Too many Christians suffer from 'cirrhosis of the giver,' you might say."

"Dis-ease leaves plenty of room for miracles," Gracie reminded them.

"More of Uncle Miltie's influence," Paul grinned. "God certainly has his work cut out for Him."

Just then, Barb Jennings entered with Estelle Livett, who was loudly objective to skateboarders in the church parking lot. Noting Barb's tight expression, Gracie decided to see if she could help calm down the domineering soprano whose talent was often at odds with her tantrums.

"Estelle, I don't know if I told you how much I enjoyed the All-County concert. Your solo was lovely." Gracie's praise was genuine.

Barb looked gratefully at her.

"Well, I wish this choir would do more sophisticated pieces—ones that would take better advantage of my unique talent," Estelle snapped back. "But thank you."

Estelle eyed Barb. "My teacher, as I've told you, was

adamant that I turn professional." She gave a sad sigh. "But it was not to be. So, I guess, my work with other groups like the All-County have to be where I come into my own—Lord knows our little choir is just not challenging enough for me or enough of a showcase."

Barb chose to say nothing, though Gracie could sense her mounting irritation.

"We're fortunate that you consent to participate, then."

Paul now decided to intervene. To the choir director, the minister said, "I especially appreciate those preludes. You've created a nice blend of traditional, contemporary and classical pieces."

"She often gets lucky when she matches voices and personalities to the anthems," Estelle conceded magnanimously.

Marge now looked at Barb and winked. "As long as we have Estelle to set such an example of musical perfection, then we choir members can only consider ourselves not just fortunate, but honored."

"Why, thank you, Marge," Estelle said.

Gracie looked gratefully at her best friend, who wore an impish expression.

Pastor Paul now hastily changed the subject. "I sometimes turn a blind eye to those boys in the parking lot. They really don't have any place to go, since most of the businesses in town have banned them from their macadam."

"Do you blame them?" Estelle certainly didn't.

"I stay out of their way, I admit," Marge acknowledged. "But as far as I can tell, they've never caused any problems. There's been no vandalism, has there?"

Paul confirmed there hadn't, and that the boys once in a while helped him with odd jobs around the church. "They don't show up until after school, usually only stay about an hour or so and then disappear—I suppose to eat supper."

"They frighten me a little," Barb conceded. "You read about boys like that in the paper. Usually too late, that is, once they've done something horrible."

"And don't think I didn't hear those comments they made when I got out of my car today," Estelle said.

Marge tried to hide her amusement. Estelle was more than a few pounds overweight, and could barely navigate the narrow steps to the choir loft without several rest stops to catch her breath.

"They have no respect," Barb said. "That's the problem."

"You're right." Pastor Paul was always ready to seize the moment, eager to transform calamity into opportunity. "Those kids just need some willing mentors—supportive folks to encourage them to channel their talents in the right direction." He looked at his parishioners. "Respect is something to be *earned*. I know you all understand that."

He was pointing them in the direction of involvement,

Gracie now understood. She remembered aloud how Chuckie Moon had blossomed under the tutelage of Officer Jim Thompson, Harry Durant and Pastor Paul.

"And your vote of confidence helped," Marge reminded her.

Paul nodded. "Mentors can make all the difference. Harry did more than hire a part-time apprentice mechanic with Chuckie, he practically adopted a son. Why, he's taken on more than a half dozen of Willow Bend's troubled boys, as I hear it, even with a family of his own. There's a mark of character!"

They all agreed that the town's garage owner had taken certain teenagers under his wing when no one else was willing to trust them.

"Love of cars is the tie that binds, in their case," Marge said. "It was Chuckie's passion for that car he was restoring that Harry responded to. He gave him space, both literally and figuratively. And so Chuckie got back on track. I hear he's applying to colleges."

"So," Paul concluded, "caring intervention can make a difference. What do you say we corral a few more wayward sheep?"

"What do you have in mind?" This came from Gracie, who understood her pastor must already have a plan.

"I discovered that three of the boys are in a band. When they're not out with their boards, they practice in Tim Weaver's garage. They call themselves the Benders." Paul eyed Barb. "From what I've heard, they're not bad—it sounds like music, not just noise!"

Estelle crossed her arms, but said nothing.

"A couple of them stay on the periphery of the youth group," Paul told them. "Sometimes they join us for excursions and social activities, but I haven't been able to get any of them to Sunday school. Now that Chuckie's coming regularly, though, maybe we could use his example—and their musical interests—as a way of bringing them closer to God."

Gracie knew it was probably a passion for something other than the Scriptures—and not cars, either—that had brought Chuckie Moon to Sunday school. But, still, whether it was Amy Cantrell or a genuine desire to learn, God would use the opportunity to transform a heart. And it was quite evident that He was doing just that in the life of one of Willow Bend's most decidedly unpredictable teens.

Marge agreed. "Now that he's a member of Eternal Hope, he's the perfect candidate to act as an example to the younger boys. That I can see."

Paul grinned. "More than that. I've recruited both Chuckie and Amy to help launch our new Youth Outreach program." He paused. "If it's all right with all of you, that is?"

Gracie held her breath. She looked at their choir director.

"Well, I hope you're not suggesting we make some musical use of those delinquents. I've not only had to jump out of their way in the parking lot, but I've also heard the bass blaring from their cars tooling around town!" Barb's impatience was evident.

Paul simply looked at her, his expression serene.

"Well, I'll think about it. This may be one time I'd have to agree with Estelle that I'm not musically 'sophisticated' enough!"

Everyone laughed. Estelle, however, appeared worried. "How do you plan on reconciling the hideous, tuneless music these kids listen to with ours, provided you can even get them involved?"

Paul had obviously been pondering this very problem, figuring out the best way to bring together the varied participants without pitched conflict. "We'll just have to warm everyone up to the idea." He paused. "My real objective is to try a special youth-led Saturday night service. If it's a success, we can decide how frequently to hold it."

"You can't expect much from heathens," Estelle warned.

Paul's smile was gentle. "If you mean teenagers, then let me remind you, Jesus looked at people and saw them for what they were."

Gracie was proud of her pastor. When others had judged by outward appearance, Jesus had looked to the heart. He saw a great Gospel writer in a tax collector, and evangelists in a pair of fishermen. And Paul the pastor endeavored to follow suit.

Estelle heaved a sigh. "I suppose it *is* our Christian duty.

And it probably is better having them inside the church than outside, scaring off potential members with their hooliganism. Swooping and smashing all around our parking lot!"

Gracie thought of something. Quoting a well-loved family rule, she told them, "No matter how crusty a person is, on the inside there is always some cream filling!"

All three stared at her.

"What I mean," she explained, "is that each of us has good qualities, if we only have the faith to understand that they may not be immediately apparent."

She took a breath. "I know how we sometimes overlook that fact when we're angry or afraid. I'm guilty, too. I once judged Chuckie and his friends by the color of their hair and their body piercings." After all, she herself had long been in quest of a certain elusive shade of vibrant red, so she cheerfully admitted, "We all struggle to find our own identity. You can't fault a person for their choice of hair color. I agree that for the sake of all the young people here in town we need a contemporary service—something they can get involved with, even take *charge* of."

She smiled at Paul. "It's a wonderful idea."

"Thank you, Gracie," he said, "for your eloquent support."

Estelle put a hand up. "Do you have any specific plan— a way to involve these scamps without creating havoc?"

"I'm sure he does," Barb ventured. Although the choir director was often tentative and self-critical, she did truly love music. It was her gift to be able to elicit a virtuoso performance from the most timid of choristers. Gracie was confident Barb wouldn't be able to help warming to the challenge that these young people presented.

"I was hoping to introduce the possibility at the later service, since most of the younger families and teenagers attend that one." Pastor Paul smiled, his eyes sparkling at the prospect. "What I'd like is to offer one piece of music that will bring to bear everyone's talents—and love of the Lord."

The choir director nodded thoughtfully. "I read not long ago how some pop music takes traditional compositions and reworks them. That might be a way to go. I'm willing to try if they are!"

"But we will have to be careful choosing music," Estelle warned. "Nothing sacrilegious." She was not to be unseated as self-appointed queen of the choir loft. She gave a snap of her chin. "I'd be willing to work with them," she went on, "as long as we have an understanding. *I* am the one with musical training, after all. I could teach them a few things!"

Estelle then set her sights on Paul. "You'll be sure to give them a lecture on civility and courtesy toward their elders?"

"My dear ladies," their pastor said, with the flourish of an imaginary hat, "you can count on me."

THE CHOIR'S FIRST PRACTICE with the Benders, who had agreed to try out the collaboration, was scheduled for several nights later. Barb waited for Gracie in the church parking lot. "Paul is in there now—with four of them."

She wrung her hands. "Oh, Gracie! These are kids—teenagers! There's no way I can handle them!"

"You'll be fine." Gracie tried to sound optimistic. Secretly, however, she could only cross her fingers.

Barb went on fussing, "I suppose I'll have to transpose our music into all kinds of different keys." Her expression was stricken. "Why, oh why, did I agree to this?" She was a born worrier.

"Because you have a good heart." Gracie told her with an encouraging smile. "Let's give God a chance, okay?"

Gracie glanced heavenward. *You're our Troubadour, Lord. Help us make this musical journey one that rings with Your praises.*

Barb reached for the door. "Well, I guess it's time to face the music."

Gracie patted her friend on the back and followed her into the church.

Pastor Paul met them at the door to the sanctuary. Several of the other choir members were sitting in the back pews. Gracie scanned the group, trying to gauge their different moods.

Marybeth Bower looked uncertain, but not uncooperative. Lester Twomley played with his glasses. Was it because he couldn't believe what he was seeing? Gracie hoped not. She glanced at the kids. Nothing too out of the ordinary—baggy pants, oversized T-shirts. Okay, the African American boy had lemon-yellow hair. He could outgrow it, Gracie reasoned. Chuckie had.

Rick Harding, their reliably upbeat tenor, leaned back against the pew, arms crossed, watching the band set up. He grinned when he saw Gracie. "Pretty cool, huh?"

He pointed toward the large rectangular boxes sprouting cables and connected to various electronic gadgets. "Now those woofers pack a howl!"

"Glory be! Look at the size of those amplifiers!" Barb exclaimed.

This would definitely make for a change of pace, Gracie thought. In fact, it was almost like time travel, from a past era to a future one, and all in the space of a second! She took a deep breath. Pastor Paul and the kids needed her respect. This was outreach in the very best sense, and she intended now to help set an example for the others.

"I want to be optimistic, but . . ." Barb looked at Rick, "do they really need *all* that?"

Rick shrugged. "Can't hurt. Myself, I'm all for raising the roof. Didn't the Lord say to make a joyful noise?"

"There's the spirit!" Paul laughed.

"They'll rock the sanctuary, that's for sure," Lester said.

"Or blow out a few hearing aids!" Estelle said, coming up behind them.

Paul guided Rick down front to meet the kids.

Tish and Tyne arrived behind Estelle. Known as the Turner twins, they were inseparable, still dressed alike and finished each other's sentences more often than not. This, despite the fact that both were happily married and lived on opposite sides of town.

Tish pointed to the boy tightening a pair of cymbals. "Isn't that . . . ?"

"Quasi Weaver," Tyne finished. "He's had more flavors of hair color than KoolAid."

Tish lowered her voice. "And that's the Knight girl. Jackie, my babysitter, says she's headed for trouble. Smoking, chasing boys."

Don Delano now sat down and craned his neck. "Ahh! And there's the Miller boy! Chad owes me a couple of back assignments. And it's Ashley Knight, and Cedric Owens, too! Thank you, pastor," he called to Paul. "You've delivered three of my favorite whiz kids right into my hands!" Don rubbed his hands together, grinning.

He got up and headed down the aisle. His fellow choir members watched the high school science teacher with curiosity.

"Um, er, Mr. Delano!" Cedric's eyes widened in surprise.

"You're probably wondering where my assignment is," Chad said, as Don approached them.

Don crossed his arms. "I guess your python ate it."

"Huh?" Chad glanced toward Cedric and rolled his eyes.

"He doesn't have a python," Cedric answered for him.

Don continued. "No? Then do you have a dog?"

Chad shifted his weight from one foot to the other.

"Sure . . . but, Mr. Delano, my *dog* didn't eat my homework!"

"Good! Then I'll expect to see it on my desk in the morning."

"Hey, Mr. Delano, how are you? I like your jacket." Ashley now batted her eyelashes.

"Well, thank you, but we need, still, to talk about your grade, okay? Tonight, though, we're here to sing praises to the Lord." Don smiled.

Marge, meanwhile, had joined Gracie at the front of the church, where Barb was trying to determine where they would stand.

"How about a semicircle?" Marge suggested, moving to show the choir director how it would look. "Right here, behind the band."

"This is going to be great!" Paul enthused. Gracie hoped he was right.

The kids were still tuning when Barb cleared her throat, and tapped on her music stand with a pencil. "Practice begins punctually at seven."

She glanced toward the band. "And ends promptly at eight. Timeliness is next to godliness!"

Pastor Paul took his place in the front pew, as Amy Cantrell bolted down the aisle. He stood to meet her.

"I've got the posters! The youth group just finished them today after school. We called a special meeting, because I thought you'd want to publicize it as soon as possible. We've even included tear-off invitations to church, with the time of the service and everything."

Now Pastor Paul addressed the group before him. "I want to thank the choir for going along with me on this. Eternal Hope may be a church with a fine history, but nothing is static, least of all a living, breathing congregation like this one. Now let the music begin!"

He spread his hands out in welcome, then sat down. The rehearsal started with a tap of Barb's pencil, and soon the rafters were ringing with the combined joyful voices and instruments. There was an atmosphere of pleased triumph in the air that seemed to be mutual, band and choir alike sharing a sense of true accomplishment.

"That was great, didn't you think, Amy?" Gracie asked as she put her music down. Even Barb looked satisfied.

"Let me introduce you! There wasn't time before, with Barb's strictness about starting on schedule!" Amy giggled, then went on, "It's Chad Miller on drums, Cedric Owens on bass and Ashley Knight on keyboard. You know her mom, Darla, maybe."

Ashley's smile was hard to read; she seemed embarrassed by Amy's accolades. Gracie studied the girl. She was well dressed, it was true, but there was an unexpected certainty about her. Not at all the personality Gracie had imagined as ringleader.

"We're lucky to get her," Amy was saying. "Because she's got a great voice, too."

Then she flashed a quick grin at the light-skinned African American. "And you name the instrument, Cedric can play it! He's the original jack-of-all-music!"

"Yeah, but Quasi's pretty versatile, too. He'll fill in on acoustic guitar," Cedric was quick to inform them.

"Quasi's really good on sax, too," Amy added. "He plays in a popular jazz band. Tonight he had to work. But he's trying to get his schedule changed. We hope he'll talk his boss at Tune Time in the mall into letting him off Thursdays."

Timothy Weaver, better known as Quasi, occasionally dropped in on the Down Under, the basement hangout of the youth group. Gracie knew him better than she did the others, whom she recognized only by sight.

"Timothy's a friend of Charles Moon," Marge reminded the others. "That's the young man who waits for Amy these days on Sunday mornings."

Gracie added, "Quasi, Chuck and their friend Martin have made themselves quite helpful to some of the seniors, volunteering to do odd jobs, and help with heavy lifting."

"That young man *has* come a long way," Marge offered. "You've been a good influence on Charles, Amy."

"Charles is a really good person. He's had some trouble, but now he's turned himself around." Amy looked at Gracie. "Thanks to you, and to Pastor Paul. Hammie Miller, too."

Gracie looked pleased. "I'm proud of any part I might have played in his decision to go to college."

Amy beamed. "Now we just have to cross our fingers for him."

"Well," said Cedric, "this was pretty all right. I'm glad we agreed to try it. My parents think it's really great."

"Mine, too," Chad admitted.

Soon, Lester and Don left together, while Rick went off to the church office with Pastor Paul. Estelle asked Marge for a lift home. Marybeth Bower, Bert Benton and the others waved good night.

Barb, Gracie was happy to see, was deep in conversation with Chad and Ashley. Raising her hand in an unseen good-bye, she passed, humming, into the night.

Late the next afternoon, when Gracie arrived at the Cantrell home to leave a surprise batch of Amy's favorite peanut-butter cookies, she met, instead, Laura Clayton, who lived next door. Gracie was fond of the girl, whose auburn tresses almost matched her own. Laura charged at life with the tenacity of a quarterback, and she was fiercely protective of little sister Patsy.

"Amy isn't here," Laura told her. She was sitting on the Cantrells' front steps.

Gracie sat down beside her. "I know she loves these, so I made a batch just to say thank you for the way her presence lifts up the choir. Did she tell you how we're working with Quasi Weaver's band?"

Laura nodded. "That is *so* great. And Amy really is special. The choir loves her and so does my family. Everytime she comes over to cheer up Patsy, it makes such a big difference!"

Everyone in the Eternal Hope prayer chain had seen

the younger Clayton sister through a succession of heart-wrenching operations.

Gracie regarded her companion. Laura had had to adjust to a new household only a little more than a year after her mother died of cancer. Soon after Jack, her father, married Marilyn, Patsy soon was born, with all of her health problems.

It was to Marilyn's and Jack's credit, with the addition of Laura's generous spirit, that this family seemingly had steered clear of the turbulent waters the Nickolsons now were navigating with Katie.

"Amy was Patsy's angel, for sure. But she made all the difference to me, too. I miss her." Laura looked suddenly too serious.

Gracie studied the child. "Amy hasn't gone anywhere, dear. She lives right next door."

"She's busy now with her job at the deli," Laura explained. "And thinking about college. She says she'll have more time in the spring, and maybe we can hang out a little more, like the old days. But the truth is, she's got the choir and all that school work and enough friends her own age. Not to mention boyfriends!"

Gracie smiled at the outburst. She remembered once feeling this way about an older neighbor, a girl called Della Robbins.

"Amy came over almost every day and we'd sit on my swing and talk and talk," Laura continued. "I could tell her anything—even things I can't tell my mom." Laura paused. "She usually has enough on her mind, anyway, Patsy needing so much attention and all. I didn't want to pile all my worries on her. Amy understood. . . ."

Gracie suspected that to Amy this relationship was more casual than it had been to Laura. The older girl had no way of knowing how large her companionship loomed in the life of her younger neighbor.

Gracie put her hand on the girl's shoulder. "I'm sure Amy doesn't mean to neglect you—or Patsy—for that matter."

"I do understand—really I do. I just miss her. And Patsy doesn't need me so much anymore, either."

"Why don't *you* take these cookies." Gracie handed her the colorful tin. "Share them with Amy. Tell her they're a gift from me—and save a couple for your little sister."

Laura brightened. "That's nice. Maybe, just for a little while, we can be the way we used to be!"

"Things are never quite as they used to be," Gracie told her gently. "But they can still be memorable, if you're always open for new and wonderful things to happen."

Laura looked thoughtful. "My mother says I depended on Amy too much."

"Your mother wants what's best for you."

"But it's hard. I want a real friend—someone like Amy. Someone my age who likes me just the way I am."

"Maybe you're not giving them a chance."

"Maybe . . ."

"Making friends is hard for most people, Laura dear. All of us have handicaps of one kind or another. Some are camouflaged—hurts of heart or soul. We're all vulnerable, and making friends is risky business. *None* of us wants to get hurt."

She met Laura's gaze. "A simple 'hello' can be all the opening you need. Maybe there's another shy girl waiting for an invitation for friendship."

"I used to think that was Katie Nickolson, but that was before she started hanging around with Ashley Knight and her friends."

She could tell that Laura did not care for those older girls, but she wasn't going to say anymore. Gracie asked her, instead, what characteristics she looked for in a friend.

"Someone quiet like me. Someone who likes math and science." Laura hesitated. "Well, maybe she doesn't have to *love* math like me. Maybe she doesn't even have to *like* it. I could learn to like history, I suppose. If the person was nice."

Gracie looked at her steadily. "Do you know anyone like that?"

"Katie's in the advanced math class, and so am I. Mrs. Southard paired us up at the beginning of the year, but kids said it wasn't fair because we were both brains, even if we were younger. Ashley Knight is in the same class. She insisted Katie be her partner—so she can copy her work."

"I hope that's not true."

Laura shrugged. "Ashley brags about it. She says she never studies. She has special friends in every class."

Gracie remembered the scene in the mall. *Lord, hold on to Your precious children. Don't give up on this one.*

"I don't suppose Katie is looking for a friend now, anyway," Laura said. "She's with the most popular group in school."

"She may need a friend like you."

"Like me?"

Gracie hugged Laura again. "Someone who will love her just the way she is."

Gracie silently thanked God for this possible answer to her prayer. Katie needed a friend. Someone to encourage her to do the right thing and stay on the right path. She felt a tug. Didn't Ashley need the same kind of friend? *Certainly, Lord.*

As she stood to leave, Gracie noticed the ground around an apple tree covered with ripe red apples. "Apple dumplings!" At the same time she registered that a man was walking up Jess Horton's sidewalk.

"Huh?" Laura stood to see where Gracie was looking.

"Do you suppose your mother would mind if I pick some?"

Laura shook her head. "We don't even use them. Actually, we're not even sure whose they really are. The tree makes the border on that side between us and the Hortons. Can I help?"

Laura tossed apples to Gracie, who put them in the plastic bucket she kept in the trunk of Fannie Mae.

Gracie was scrambling to retrieve the little red globes Laura gently tossed her way. "Wasn't it in *Alice in Wonderland* that they played the funny croquet?"

"Those poor card soldiers!" Laura kicked out with her foot, sending a rotten apple sailing against the tree trunk. "'Off with their heads!' she declared."

It was then that Gracie suddenly noticed Jess looking out the window. Who was her visitor? Gracie wondered. Why wasn't she at work? And why, if she saw Gracie watching back, hadn't she waved?

GRACIE HAD JUST PARKED HER CAR at home when Rocky's little black sedan zipped in behind her. She watched as he unfolded himself from the car and tucked his rumpled Oxford-cloth shirt into his pants. He was missing a button, as usual.

"Bring that by tomorrow and I'll fix it," she said, pointing at the missing button.

"All it needs is a safety pin. Safety pins, rubber bands and duct tape: all the tools a guy needs to get by."

"Tell that to Uncle Miltie." Gracie laughed. "He can't resist a tool sale. We might as well call him Uncle Gadget!"

"Speaking of which, I hear you're getting terrible reception with that dish."

"*He's* the one with terrible reception. I just listen to him complain."

"Well, I hope I'm not about to get a terrible reception," Rocky joked.

"I guess it depends on what brings you to this end of town," Gracie told him, smiling.

He followed her into the house through the back door. "I figured I could get here just in time for your uncle's night-time snack."

"Oh," said Gracie. "It's apple dumplings—one of Aunt Doris's recipes."

"Your aunt always served it warm." Uncle Miltie commented, ambling into the kitchen. "Topped with a big scoop of French vanilla ice cream or whipped cream."

"A *small* dollop," Gracie conceded. "This *is* your second helping this evening."

Uncle Miltie gave a good-natured chuckle. "You know, you're sounding more and more like your aunt all the time!"

"It's a female thing," Rocky told him. "My wife was always fussing over me, going on about my blood pressure and cholesterol. She reminded me that diabetes ran in my family every time I so much as looked at something sweet— never mind the fact that the only recorded case was my great-great-grandfather on my mother's side!"

Gracie cut half a dumpling for herself. "You two should appreciate all that concern."

"We do, we do!" Uncle Miltie exclaimed. "It's just that too much of it and a man starts to feel . . . smothered!"

"And we don't care a lick for dieting, either!" Rocky added.

Uncle Miltie grinned. "Dieting is the penalty for exceeding the *feed* limit."

Rocky and Gracie both laughed. "Okay," Gracie shot back. "I'll try to go easy with the smother love. I probably worry about you more than I should. But, if *I'm* not going to, who is?"

She scanned the pair. Rocky's shaggy salt-and-pepper hair was in need of cutting. She reached over to fix Uncle Miltie's collar. "It's evident the two of you don't pay much attention to diet—or exercise, for that matter."

"Hey, hey! I'm in shape," Rocky protested.

Uncle Miltie rolled his eyes. "*Round's* a shape."

Gracie felt things were getting a little too personal and decided to change the subject.

"How's it going with Pastor Paul's new career as a columnist?"

"That's why I stopped over. I've got a piece to run this week—Paul's, as you know—but Jess is drawing a blank for the next one. She simply hasn't had any other response from local clergy to our plea for contributions."

Rocky took a gulp of his coffee. "Gracie, maybe you could help her. We sent all the churches an announcement that we were launching a page that would feature a weekly column, along with an invitation to contribute. As of now, though, Paul's been the only volunteer we've roped in."

Gracie thought a moment. "I'm catering the annual Mason County Ecumenical Luncheon in a few days, I'll talk it up there."

"That would be great." Rocky pushed his last bite of dumpling around in the bowl. "And . . . I know you'll still be thinking about what we discussed about Jess."

"Is something else the matter?" Gracie said anxiously, somehow guessing that there was.

"She's requested time off. But with no explanation. Just says it's a personal matter. The thing is, she knows I'm already aware of some of the problems she's facing."

"Maybe it's something with her kids," Uncle Miltie suggested. "They're always catching one thing or another."

Rocky shrugged. "I can give her some leeway, but she has to talk to me."

"That girl needs a church family," Uncle Miltie decided. "If the kids are sick, we can lend a hand with child care. And if it's something else, well," her uncle smiled, "prayer has a way of fixing what ails a person."

Gracie agreed. "I've been praying for her and her family."

"Sounds like the Lord's answering," her uncle said. "He's calling on you, Gracie, to befriend her."

"Gracie, I know you've got a lot on your plate right now. Don't worry about finding a literary-minded minister for me—keeping that prayerful eye on Jess is more important." Rocky looked at her fondly.

"Rocky, that's really quite thoughtful of you. But I enjoy problem-solving. Of all kinds. It keeps me feeling involved . . . and needed. It'll be no trouble to collar a few clergymen at the lunch, and, of course, Jess Horton's still on my docket!"

Gracie studied Patsy's mother from the other side of Claytons' kitchen table. She had set out to call on Jess. But when Jess didn't answer her bell, Gracie went next door to call on the Claytons. Now, she realized that here was most likely where she was suppose to be. Silently, she thanked God for guiding her.

Marilyn was a pretty woman with a usually bright smile. She normally put people at ease with her hospitality, but this morning she seemed preoccupied.

She did have her hands full with Patsy's disability, Gracie thought. She laced her fingers around the warm teacup. A discussion of the investment club would have to wait. This friend also needed her. She prayed there weren't any new problems with Patsy's health, for Laura had mentioned none.

"Laura told me she intercepted you when you stopped by next door," Marilyn said. "She enjoyed helping you pick apples."

Gracie thanked her for allowing her to take them. "I was looking for Amy but was delighted to find Laura, instead. She's a great girl."

"Yes, she's been a real trooper through all of Patsy's

difficulties. I sometimes feel we neglect her, but she seems happy on her own, most of the time. And now that Patsy's doing so well—we're so proud of her. She's truly an inspiration to us all. But . . . lately, Laura's been a bit down."

Gracie wondered out loud if it had something to do with Amy's being so busy, making Laura feel neglected by yet another person.

"Laura loves Amy," Marilyn agreed. "And Amy, as you know, dotes on Patsy. Laura was satisfied to bask in the overspill. But Amy's got her life to live. I've explained to Laura how friendships wax and wane and how seeing less of a friend doesn't necessarily mean they care for you less. They may just find their life suddenly busy in new ways."

"That's very wise," Gracie said. "But it simply may be hard for Laura to accept the change."

Gracie then told her about Laura's interest in Katie as a friend. At that point, Gracie felt she could comfortably move on to broach the subject of the Kidnappers Club. From Phyllis and Darren it was but a short leap.

"I've been thinking about pulling out," Marilyn said. "I'm just so busy with Patsy and my volunteer work at the nursing home. You know, I play checkers every week with Tex Stevenson—what an adorable man! And not any less sharp at ninety-five than he was at eighty-five!"

Marilyn looked at Gracie's picnic basket on the counter. "I should get one of those. They're so old-fashioned—I think the folks I visit would appreciate it, seeing a real basket when I take them little homemade treats, instead of a paper shopping bag."

Marilyn paused, and Gracie waited. Her companion shrugged and took a sip of tea. "I guess stocks and bonds aren't so intriguing anymore."

Gracie searched her friend's eyes. "Everything else is okay?"

"Finances have been a little tight. What with Patsy's medical bills, and all, it's a tight stretch. I'm simply feeling the strain."

She managed a proud smile. "But the financial bind is only temporary, until we get on top of these medical bills."

"I hear you and Jess have become good friends," Gracie said, thinking it a good moment for changing the subject again.

"You're a very good neighbor, Gracie. Jess told me that you reached out to her, offering to help in any way you can. We're lucky to have you in Willow Bend. And I know you've heard her concerns about the club's bookkeeping." Marilyn poured more tea for Gracie. "She also said that she asked you for help in solving this problem. She may not have lived here long, but she somehow knew that was the right thing to do."

"It's probably going to turn out to be a minor error in entering figures that created the discrepancy. I understand that's what Darla Knight thinks."

"That's probably what she told Jess." The sharp tone of Marilyn's voice surprised Gracie. "Darla likes being in charge. Selling real estate suits her."

"What makes you say that?"

Marilyn shrugged it off. "Oh, sometimes it's just she comes on a little strong for me. I probably shouldn't have said anything."

"But if it has something to do with the current unresolved situation. . . ."

"Listen, Gracie," Marilyn began, "it's really great you're helping with this. I dislike being caught in the middle—especially now that Jess and I are becoming closer."

"Darla said something else to you?"

"Not to me—to Phyllis, and Marybeth. Actually, I think I'm the first and last one in the group to know most things." Marilyn stirred her tea. "Jess called me the night she discovered the discrepancy. So I walked over to her house, and we pored over the receipts until almost midnight. Nothing. We've been carrying a balance six hundred dollars short of what the deposits say we should have. At first, I thought it was caused by one of our less prudent investments—a couple of them were big losers in the last market downturn."

"And now?" Gracie sensed the woman's reluctance. "Just what is it Darla's saying?"

"That Jess has financial problems. Darla found out while talking real estate to someone indiscreet at the bank. It seems Jess had some trouble securing a loan."

Gracie frowned. It was unfortunate that the discussion had turned so intrusive, and possibly damaging, to Jess's

CHURCH CHOIR MYSTERIES

reputation. It went against her every instinct, but she had to have all the information if she was going to figure out what had gone wrong with the books.

"The discrepancy appeared in the last quarter, Gracie—which Darla was all too quick to point out. And Jess is our newest member."

"Do you believe she took the money?"

Marilyn shook her head. "Jess was a basket case when I went over to her house that night. She was so worried. We went over and over those books, and the more clear it became the money was not there, the more Jess fussed. She was the one to bring it to our attention. That's what I told Darla. If she'd taken it, keeping silent would make more sense."

"Do you have any idea who would take the money?"

Marilyn shook her head. "We were all friends."

Gracie caught the past tense. "And now?"

"Well, what I do know is that Phyllis and Darla have been talking. Marybeth overheard them, because she told me, too. She says that Betsey Griswold knows, as well. The implication is that Jess could have fabricated the mistake in the books."

Gracie's heart sunk.

"So, you see, I'm also the last one to know. I think it's because Jess and I are now closer friends. And I also think it's because Darla has to run the show. I don't want to presume ill of her, really I don't, but it really looks as if she's been planting doubt, suggesting dishonesty, behind Jess's back. And the worst part is that she hasn't given Jess the opportunity to defend herself."

Marilyn went on to explain that, over the years, the group had agreed to purchases of teaching materials, videotapes and a computer program; and they were not always careful to keep records, often paying the purchaser without a receipt.

"We've had quite a few speakers, though most probably donated their time. For a long time, we operated with cash, giving money to members to make purchases. Sometimes it was for refreshments, or occasionally to send flowers when someone was sick or grieving. We really didn't keep track. It would be relatively easy to embezzle money from the club."

"I don't like what I'm thinking," Gracie told her, "but this is starting to sound like shortages could have been there for a long time, maybe accumulating only now to something this noticeable."

There was a long pause. Marilyn looked grim. "The problem really is, I think Jess has been framed."

Gracie's eyes widened. "Framed?" she said, her distress obvious.

"That's the part I hate the most—thinking that one of my friends was stealing from us. We've been together all this time, and we've shared a thousand cups of coffee and as many tears—some of sorrow, more in joy. The Kidnappers have been a close group, Gracie. So I hate suspecting anything, but I really believe it to be true. As I look back, I remember other times when the books didn't seem quite right. We questioned it then, but went ahead and chalked up the discrepancies to sloppy bookkeeping."

She met Gracie's gaze. "You see, before, it was ten or twenty dollars. And we weren't bothering with receipts."

"This is truly a terrible situation!" Gracie exclaimed. "Most of the club goes to church with me. I don't want to think one of you isn't honest, but for everyone's sake we *must* get at the truth. If someone is stealing, she needs help. The group has the responsibility to confront her—to bring her back to the right path."

"I'm awfully glad you're involved now, Gracie. What can I do to help you?"

Gracie got out a little notebook. "You said that the club buys all its stocks through an Internet company?"

"Yes, a couple of years ago, we discovered an online broker. Darla turned us on to that, because her husband was using one."

Marilyn reached for the teapot to pour again, but Gracie declined. "I really have to go shortly. Lots of errands and appointments. And maybe Jess will be home now."

Marilyn stood up to look out her kitchen window. "Her car is in the driveway. You say you knocked?"

"At both doors." Gracie moved to stand beside Marilyn. They stood in silence, both lost in their own thoughts, and neither liking what the other was probably thinking. *Lord, I'm worried about her.*

Marilyn turned to face her. She attempted to change the direction of their thinking.

"You know, Gracie, if you and Marge are serious about starting an investment club, Internet investing is the way to go. Easy, no load, just a flat fee. You can run your checking account out of the same company.

"Terry Nickolson is our expert on tap. He actually set our account up, and at first, he purchased the stocks for us. The last couple months we started taking turns. *I've* actually done it." Marilyn smiled. "And if I can do it, anyone can."

That was the same thing Wendy had concluded about computing. She bought one to keep the books for her dance studio, and to enhance Elmo's education. Her artistic daughter-in-law was one of the last people Gracie would have expected to embrace technology.

It struck Gracie suddenly that Terry obviously had access to investment club books. Terry, who had recently bought a six hundred dollar knife. Maybe she could try and learn about online brokerage services, after all. It would be the perfect opportunity to get to know the man better, and to hear if it sounded like he had anything to hide.

Marilyn walked her to the door. "Gracie, I'd appreciate your keeping us in your prayers. Laura needs to come out of herself—she's so much in that world of her own. In her mind, anyway, Amy Cantrell is still her closest friend. But I'll get in touch with Phyllis, about Katie, too. I just haven't wanted to deal with this thing." She gave a faint smile. "I guess I just hoped it would go away—or better yet, solve itself."

Gracie promised she would pray for the family.

Now, Lord, where next?

T HE NEXT MEETING of the Kidnappers Club was being held at Marybeth Bower's home. The children gathered happily in the family room with popcorn and videos. Ashley and Katie, being older, were missing.

Marge had showed up with bells on, almost literally. Gracie glanced at her always unpredictable friend sitting next to her: from Marge's ears jingled little silver dollar signs, in honor of the event. Gracie could solve many mysteries, but she could never detect ahead of time what her friend's accessories might be.

"I bought my first investment magazine," Marge now whispered to Marilyn, on the other side of her. "Dabbling in the market has a certain dangerous ring to it. I can't *wait* to get started."

Marilyn smiled absently, and Gracie felt her strain. She

sensed it had nothing to do with Marge's exuberance, however, but rather with the presence at the other end of the table. She looked down the dining table to where Darla was going over the agenda with Phyllis and their guest speaker.

Betsey Griswold chatted with Marybeth about her choice of unusual seasonings for the spice cake she'd served. Jess was the only member missing.

"Have you talked to Jess?" Gracie quietly asked Marilyn.

Marilyn shook her head. "A man left her house shortly after you went home. I happened to see him when I was out in the yard." Her smile brightened. "You made me feel guilty about wasting those apples, so I was gathering a few for applesauce. When I saw him leave, I walked over to the fence to talk to Jess. I'm sure she saw me, but she turned and went back inside without saying anything. I must have been mistaken."

Gracie remembered the man she'd seen the day before.

"I think the kids are sick," Marilyn went on. "I haven't seen them in the yard. So, maybe he was a doctor—I didn't recognize him, though." Marilyn hesitated. "Although, he didn't look like a doctor. He seemed angry. Maybe you should drop over again tomorrow and see if she answers the door. I'd go, but I'm afraid she'd think I was prying."

"You're too good friends for that." Gracie patted her hand. "But I will make it a point to try and see her tomorrow. Rocky had told me she'd asked for time off."

"I don't think she went to work today, either." Marilyn met her gaze. "I'm getting more worried about her, Gracie."

Gracie did not like to admit that she was feeling the same way.

Darla called the meeting to order and introduced the speaker, a woman from a brokerage in Mason City. Marge scribbled notes feverishly as she heard about the ins and outs of long-term care insurance and protecting assets from being devoured by medical expenses.

Gracie chewed her pencil.

Six-year-old Bobby answered the door when Gracie called on Jess. His scab-pocked face revealed the probable reason for Jess's absence from work—chicken pox.

"Gracie, come in," Jess called from behind her son.

Their house was furnished with a mixture of antique belongings and new ones, although many pieces looked hand-painted. Stacks of paperbacks, magazines and picture books were scattered about. Old photographs adorned what looked to be a player piano. Gracie walked over to look at them.

"Your home is very cozy."

Jess joined her in front of the piano. "This is grand-mother's white elephant. It's been around the family for years. No one wanted to part with it—but no one had room for it. R. J. and I ended up with it because we had the largest house, an old Victorian with nooks and crannies."

"And a scary basement," Bobby told her.

Jess ruffled his hair. "You loved it. Lots of games of hide-and-seek, huh?"

"I miss my friends."

She hugged her son. "Me, too."

"It certainly is beautiful," Gracie said, rubbing her hand over the polished mahogany. "Does it work?"

Jess nodded. "As a girl, I use to practice with the rolls, my fingers racing to keep up with the ragtime Grandma loved. It was our entertainment in the evenings. We lived with my grandmother for a while when my father was serving in the Navy—submarine duty. He was gone for months at a time."

Molly hopped on the stool. "*I* can play the piano."

"Can-*not!*" Bobby exclaimed. "You just put your fingers on the keys. The piano plays the music."

Molly hit the little button, and a Scott Joplin melody danced across the keys. Molly raced to keep up, her enthusiasm enough to exhaust them all. Her motions blended fluidly with the music. Watching the child's pudgy fingers on the keys, Gracie could almost believe she was playing.

Gracie thought of her special times with God. Those were moments when she, like Molly, simply followed her Master's lead, His music a pattern for her life.

"How about a glass of cranberry juice? Or apple?" Jess suggested when the roll ended. Molly simply hopped off the stool and dashed off ahead of her mother. "And cookies! Mommy and I made them this morning!"

"You, my cute little cookie, are going to take a nap." Jess scooped the pigtailed pre-schooler into her arms. "You ate more than your fill when were baking them."

Jess smiled at her son. "How about giving Mrs. Parks and me about an hour of quiet time? You can pop in a video for you and your sister. She'll fall asleep on the couch."

His sister wiggled out of her mother's grasp. "I won't fall asleep! I'm a big girl now! I want to pick the video."

Jess gave Molly a warning look. "You need some rest. Get your blankie, and let your brother put in the video."

"You broke the recorder the last time. You rammed the tape in upside down," Bobby reminded her.

Molly crossed her arms, and stuck out her bottom lip. "It was an accident. Mom said so herself."

"It was stupid!" Bobby glared.

"Mom!" Molly looked to her mother in indignation. "Bobby said the S word!"

The boy rolled his eyes. "I didn't call you stupid! I said it was a stupid thing to do. And it was!"

"Bobby, please!" Jess eyed him.

Bobby scowled. "She's such a baby."

"Am not."

"Are too!"

Jess positioned herself between them. "Enough. Molly get your blanket and pillow. You can pick the video, but Bobby will put it in the player, all right?"

Molly nodded, but not enthusiastically.

Bobby was about to protest when his mother shot him a warning look. "Watch the video quietly—together. Or, you can both go to your rooms and nap. Quiet time is just *that*."

"Molly's videos are boring! They put me to sleep!"

Jess smiled mischievously. "That's the whole idea."

The pair darted off in opposite directions. She watched them with loving eyes.

"Diplomacy," Jess told Gracie.

Gracie chuckled. "Looks like good parenting to me."

"Thanks. I can use all the appreciation I can get." A flush of melancholy crossed her face. "Alone can be lonely!"

"You don't have to do it that way." Gracie watched Jess putting glasses on the counter. "The offer still stands to come and experience the Eternal Hope family. I really think alone might seem less lonely then."

"So Paul says." But her tone didn't sound convinced.

Gracie wished there was something she could say or do. Grief was so much easier to bear, shared. *Oh Lord, how do we reach her?*

"The column Paul turned in is excellent," Jess said, handing a glass of juice over to Gracie.

"I'm looking forward to reading it."

There was an awkward silence.

"Paul uses some anecdotes about his relationship with his father," Jess said. "I like the way he drew a comparison to his relationship with God."

Jess looked pensive. "They were quite poignant, really. Reading his column did make me almost envy his relationship with God."

Could this be an opening? Gracie looked to heaven.

"If the truth be known, Gracie," Jess went on. "I probably am rebelling against God. He is undoubtedly waiting with perfect patience for me to come home. But right now, I'm just not ready." She sighed. "Right now, I have too much to deal with in my own life. I've got my closets to get straightened, and I can't have God poking around in every little corner, turning up every speck of dust."

Gracie wanted to tell her that God wasn't like that. In those times when she was forced to deal with the dust and clutter in her soul, God was a gentle, shining light, making it easier to restore order because His presence allowed her to see things so much more clearly.

We've come a long way, You and I, Lord. Thanks for being so patient with me.

Jess was lost in her own thoughts. Gracie searched for the right thing to say. "God understands."

"I know." The young woman's voice was barely audible.

Jess looked at Gracie. "My life is a mess, Gracie. Maybe if

I went back to New York—faced my problems. I don't know. I thought moving here was for the best. A new beginning. R. J. and I didn't have any roots in Rochester. Just his work. I'm not really close to my family, and R. J. didn't have any."

"Really, Jess, I want to help." Gracie put her hand on top of the younger woman's. "Tell me what's wrong."

Jess exhaled. "My immediate problem is your pastor. You're not Eternal Hope's only cheerleader."

"Paul means well."

"He's a lovely man, Gracie. Don't get me wrong, I don't take offense at his attempts at spiritual counseling. The problem is that I find myself attracted to him." She looked at Gracie. "I don't need another complication in my life. I can't let myself fall for your pastor, not while the kids are so young."

"Have you talked to Paul about this?" Gracie was perplexed. Hadn't the two just recently become acquainted? Perhaps Jess was projecting too much onto the relationship.

"Of course not," Jess said. "You think I'm going to tell a man I just met that I think I'm falling in love with him? I mean really, Gracie, it's so crazy! I don't understand these emotions myself." She rested her head on her hands. "I found myself uncomfortably attracted to him right off the bat. He's shy, but that's only endearing. He loves his work and all of you. He's so polite, and he listens. He's so unlike R. J.—not that R. J. didn't listen. Well, actually, he didn't. R. J. was always busy with his work. Gracie, I think I've always been a little lonely, that I always was looking for someone like Paul."

Gracie only listened.

"Paul talked about his parents serving in mission, and his desire to see Eternal Hope become more involved. His life sounded so perfect—my dream life. He mentioned future plans for a youth mission trip, and I admitted that I liked working with teens. I served as an adviser to the Cadet Girl Scouts. It's just too soon for me, Gracie. I know I'm awfully vulnerable. Bobby and Molly need me right now."

"You need each other." Gracie smiled encouragingly. "You're wise to take the time. Paul will understand."

"It's not just that." Jess paused, as if weighing her next words. "My life is too complicated. My kids need me, and I can't even be there for them right now."

Gracie gave Jess's hand a squeeze. "You're too hard on yourself. You and Paul can still be friends. He understands your predicament, really he does. He *is* a pastor, and can be a loyal friend. Talk to him about your concerns."

Jess nodded. "I know. But I can't come back to church, not now, anyway."

Gracie appreciated the woman's honesty. "God can handle your disappointment—your anger, Jess. Talk to Him, too. Please!"

"I don't know if I believe anymore."

"Let Him help you with that unbelief."

Jess shook her head, but smiled. "You're incorrigible, Gracie Parks. Just like your pastor."

"Runs in the family."

"I do like that family." Jess smiled back. "Don't give up hope on me."

"We have hope in all things. That's what faith is. It's believing the seemingly unbelievable, and living it." Gracie chuckled. "Hebrews 11:1—paraphrased by Parks."

Jess laughed, as well.

Father, put Your arms around her—let her feel Your loving presence. Help her with her unbelief. Give her wisdom, please. And give this budding relationship the benefit of Your wisdom, as well. Pastor Paul and she seem so right for each other.

Gracie chuckled inwardly, realizing she was putting the Lord in the position of a celestial matchmaker. He wouldn't mind, she decided.

"What's so amusing?" Jess's eyes sparkled. With her sprinkling of freckles and her faint dimples, the blonde editor looked more like a junior varsity cheerleader than the thirty-something widowed mother of two.

"I was imagining you and Paul. He's quite taken with you, as well. I could see it in his face when he talked about you."

Jess blushed. "It's only friendship, Gracie."

"That's what I was talking to the Lord about—protecting

and nurturing this lovely friendship the two of you have begun."

"You were praying?"

Gracie nodded.

"It *is* a conspiracy!" Jess's tone was playful. "Half your congregation must have been at Celestial City the other night—every one of them passing, less than discreetly, I might add, by our table. They all mentioned *pray*ing."

"Everything goes better with prayer," Gracie reminded her.

"I suppose it does. The people from your church are nice. Their fondness for Paul is plain to see."

"He is pretty special to us. Lots of us have taken to mothering him. He's a perfect candidate. Paul is endearingly absent-minded, and can't cook."

"He blushes cutely, too," Jess told her. "He turned beet red when anyone made jovial comments about being pleased to see him with a date. He stumbled over excuses, giving them all the more reason to speculate that there was something between us." Jess laughed. "I sensed his parishioners were loving every minute of his discomfort."

"I'm sure."

"Of course, it also means your private life isn't so private when you're a small-town minister."

"Small-town anything!" Gracie reminded her. "In case you don't know."

"Gracie," Jess warned, "if only you knew the whole truth about me. I've a got a list of sins to bury Saint Peter."

Gracie smiled. "Nothing that can't be forgiven."

Jess shrugged. "Paul is persistent, though," she said, changing the subject. "He asked me out again."

"And?" Gracie asked.

"I told him I couldn't see him. Pursuing this relationship right now isn't fair to either one of us."

She studied Jess. The young woman's soft violet eyes showed her vulnerability. Jess was angry with God, but she hadn't rejected Him. God had brought Paul and Jess together, and He was in their midst. Of that, Gracie was sure.

Pastor Paul was waiting for her after choir practice that evening. "Well, what do you think?"

"About what?" Gracie asked, wondering if he was referring to Jess, or his article in the newspaper—or to something else altogether.

"Jess—I know she's talked to you. She made her intentions quite clear," he said. "She's not looking for a romantic involvement, at least not one with me."

"I wouldn't be so sure of that, Paul." Gracie touched his arm. "Surely, you sensed her vulnerability. She's afraid of a relationship. She's got those two kids to think about. And she loved her husband very much."

He lowered his gaze. "Don't you think I know all those

things? I'd settle for a friendship. But I don't think she's ready for even that. Something is going on with her, Gracie. She won't tell me what it is, but I sense she's scared about something—and it's not just the possibility of a relationship with me."

Gracie nodded sympathetically, not wanting to betray the woman's confidence. "Stick with her, Paul. She's trying to find her way home."

They stood a moment in companionable silence.

Paul changed the subject. "What I really need to talk to you about is the band. The kids are good, aren't they? Do you think we can start planning that Saturday night youth service? So far the congregation has seemed delighted."

Gracie had to admit she'd been enjoying the change of pace. Even Estelle seemed to get into her groove with the rhythm of Quasi's sax. He'd won Barb over with his jazz rendition of "Amazing Grace."

"Everyone seems upbeat." Gracie glanced around at the choir and band members dispersing. "I think you've already proved there's real promise to the idea."

"That Ashley has quite a voice," Don Delano said, joining them as they walked out to the parking lot. "I only wish she took mitochondria as seriously as she does music. And if she doesn't get this last lab in, I'm afraid she's going to fail the grading period."

"Have you talked to her mother?" Gracie wanted to know.

He nodded. "Mrs. Knight's a busy woman—or so she's informed me. She did make time for the conference the guidance counselor called. Ashley's got problems in most of her major subjects. Sadly, *Ms.* Knight took three cell phone calls during our conference. I have an unhappy suspicion Ashley is raising Ashley."

"Perhaps I could pay a visit," Paul suggested. "They have visited here occasionally, and now that Ashley is involved, through the band, there's no reason I shouldn't get to know her family. It's not been easy since that marriage broke up."

Gracie decided that perhaps she, too, might pay a visit to the Knights, the family that seemed to be causing so much dissension among her friends. "Perhaps we could make that visit together," she told Paul. "I *am* on the Outreach Committee."

"I'll give Mrs. Knight a call when I get home." Paul took out his appointment book. "Got any particular time in mind?"

Gracie thought for a second. "There's a lot of cooking to do tomorrow morning for the Ecumenical Luncheon. Marge is coming over to help me, but we should be finished by late afternoon."

"Perhaps we could drop by after school," Paul suggested. "Maybe Ashley will be there."

Don Delano prophesied, "Ashley'll be there. Darla's probably the one you'll have trouble pinning down. It took the counselor almost a week to catch up with her. She doesn't return calls very promptly. Good luck getting her attention!"

Their pastor remained optimistic. "We'll still try and see what happens."

"RACIE! THANK GOODNESS I caught you!" It was Jim Thompson on the telephone.

Gracie motioned for Marge to take over stirring the gelatin she had on the stove. She adjusted the phone between her ear and shoulder, listening to Jim report that Ashley Knight had been caught shoplifting at the mall after school.

Her face must have registered her shock, because Marge exclaimed, "What happened? Who is it?"

Gracie covered the phone and quickly told Marge what had happened.

"Marilyn warned that that girl was headed for trouble," Marge remembered. "Was Katie with her?"

Gracie didn't know.

"Oh, dear," Marge said, looking worried. "If she was, Phyllis and Terry and Darla all are going to need our prayers."

"The gelatin needs *you* now, Marge!" Gracie pointed, responding to the smell of burnt sugar.

Then she was back to Jim. "Was Ashley alone?"

"Katie Nickolson was with her," he told her. "And two other girls."

Gracie thanked him for phoning and asked what was going to happen now. Marge poured the gelatin over the fruit, but her attention was on the phone conversation. "Where are they?"

She moved to the chair beside Gracie, trying to catch an earful. "The girls are still at the Avery police station," Gracie whispered.

Jim had had the unpleasant responsibility of telephoning their parents. The Avery sheriff was dealing with the store owners. "He's trying to talk them out of pressing charges. They are juveniles, after all, and three of the kids are first timers."

"Someone has been charged before?"

"Ashley was caught last spring, but her mother paid for the merchandise. Darla didn't want Ashley's father to know."

Gracie sent up a prayer of comfort and healing for this troubled family.

Jim now explained, his tone rueful, "This time, I had to call Wes Knight—Ashley's father—because I couldn't reach Darla. He's insisting we lock the girl up to teach her a lesson. He refused to come to the station and even talk about it."

"Oh, Lord, that poor child." Gracie's heart went out to Ashley, trying to imagine how alone she must feel at that moment, with neither parent by her side. "She's got to be scared."

"Well, she acts like a tough cookie," Jim said. "She's trying to play it cool. I'm still leaving messages for her mother."

Gracie now quickly filled Marge in on the extent of the problem, as her friend sat down beside her at the table, wiping her hands on the towel. "Ask him what we can do."

"Pray," she answered for Jim.

He heard her. "Gracie, I think that family could use friendship, too. Maybe you and Marge could go over there tomorrow, after all this is settled."

"Is the father in town?"

"It's a Chicago number."

"I can't blame the guy for being angry," Jim went on. "I'd want to throttle the kid if she were mine. But you know— I'd be there for her. Parents have got to be there for their kids, no matter what."

Those were Gracie's sentiments exactly.

Now Jim excused himself, and spoke to someone else in the room with him.

"The sheriff says he needs me, so I've got to go pretty quick. Listen, Gracie, I haven't called Terry and Phyllis yet. I was saving them until last. Terry is a close friend. I was hoping you'd call them right after me. They're going to need some spiritual support, as well. So, you and Marge have your work cut out for you. I'm going to tell them that I told you." Jim's voice was tentative. "I may take some heat with the Avery sheriff for this, but these are Willow Benders. *Our* kids. We're like family. So I feel kind of responsible for them."

"You'd call the prayer chain if there was a physical illness," Gracie reasoned. "I think you were right to call for support now."

"Let's keep this between us, okay? You, me and Marge will be prayer warriors enough for this situation—at least until word gets out on its own."

She agreed, telling him that she would call immediately, but also that she would give Phyllis the opportunity to confide in her. "I'll offer to baby-sit, so she and Terry don't have to take Darren."

"For what it's worth, the sheriff did tell me that the store owners are *not* going to press charges against Katie or the other two girls. "We're just going to give them a good scare and a long lecture, then send them home with their parents."

They could be grateful for that. "And Ashley?"

"Well, that young lady has already had the one warning. And she was apprehended with merchandise from three stores. What's worse, she gave the security guard a hard time—kicked him in the shins and tried to get away. I caught her outside of the store, and she threatened me with a lawsuit for false arrest."

Gracie closed her eyes. It was worse than she could have imagined. That uncertain-seeming young woman had a temper!

"It's pretty tough to have sympathy for that kid. But I'm working on it, Gracie. I'd appreciate your praying for us as we deal with her."

"Thanks again for calling me." She put the phone down.

"He really is one of the good guys," Marge said. "I've seen him with the kids in Willow Bend. And I for one am glad he was on special duty today over there in the mall."

She waited twenty minutes, then dialed Phyllis's number. They talked only a few minutes, with Phyllis accepting Gracie's offer to baby-sit. "You're truly a gift from God, Gracie," she told her, "only angels probably can't cook as well!"

Gracie bent to scoop up Gooseberry, explaining to him that she probably wouldn't be back for a while. "I'll leave a note for Uncle Miltie," she told Marge. "Make sure he doesn't sample the food for the luncheon."

"I'll stop back over later, after he gets back from the senior center, and fill him in," Marge said. "You get going. I can finish up here—put the food in the refrigerator with notes attached threatening that old codger with bodily harm if he so much as takes a nibble. He knows I'll check, so he'll behave himself. And, by the way, isn't Rocky coming over to make further adjustments to that contraption on your roof?"

Gracie put her hand to her head. She had completely forgotten. "He assumes he's getting supper."

"I know your freezer almost as well as I know my own. I'll call later and see how things are going with the Nickolsons. If you're not home in time, I'll feed them with something tasty. Of course, defrosting isn't synonymous with fancy, but beggars can't be choosers, right?"

Gracie hugged her friend. "You're the best."

"Wait until you get my bill." Marge grinned. "Now, you get going—that child is waiting for you. Give Darren a kiss for me!"

She waved from the back door. "And don't worry, I'll keep both the boys here in line! It's just another kind of babysitting, really!"

WHEN GRACIE ARRIVED at the Nickolsons, they
avoided discussing the problem that had brought
her there in the first place, focusing instead on Darren's routine. Phyllis's eyes were red, and Gracie wanted to put her
arms around her, but she was afraid it would unleash a
further flood of tears.

Phyllis, Gracie knew, was a proud woman, struggling to
stay strong for her family. Gracie rubbed her back for minute.
"We'll be all right—and so will Katie."

Phyllis sighed. "I hope so."

Terry paced, going over where the light switches were,
showing Gracie how to turn on the TV, and what to do in
case of an emergency. Gracie knew he was suffering, as well.

*Lord, draw them close, brace them with Your love in this difficult
time.*

While Darren was napping, Gracie called the church. True,

Jim had asked her to keep this latest episode between them, but Paul was in the business of keeping confidences. Besides, they'd been planning to visit the Knights together later that afternoon. The church secretary had told Paul she'd called Darla several times, leaving messages on both her cell and home phones.

"She goes to the gym," Paul now explained to Gracie. "Or, at least, that's what Pat thinks. She could be with a client, however, and not answering her calls."

"Try Jim first," Gracie told him. "See if he's managed to locate her. I hate the thought of Ashley's being in the Avery sheriff's office all alone. Terry and Darla just left—I presume the other parents have, as well."

Paul promised to let her know as soon as he had fresh news. Gracie checked on Darren, and then sat down with a Guideposts book. She wasn't into more than a half-dozen pages when the doorbell rang. There stood Amy Cantrell and Laura Clayton.

"We heard about Katie and Ashley from Charles," Amy explained, as Gracie ushered them into the living room. "Quasi works after school at the mall, and Charles was visiting him there. I guess Ashley was creating a pretty big ruckus."

"Quasi says, actually, pretty much everyone we know was there, hanging out," Laura added.

Amy smiled. "Not everybody—just a few kids he recognized. But you can believe everyone knows by now.

Megan Williamson was there, and she's a mega-gossip!"

"We wanted to see if there was anything we could do to help," Laura said solemnly to Gracie. "Katie is probably pretty scared, huh?"

Gracie's eyes blurred for an instant as she felt the sweet seriousness of Laura's concern. "Let's go into the kitchen," she suggested.

Over milk and cookies, Amy offered a few more details, and she confirmed that Ashley had been rude to the store owner, kicking the security guard and resisting as Jim very reasonably tried to take her into custody.

"Charles figured I'd want to know, since they were planning to practice tonight—just the band."

Laura wiped off a slight milk moustache with a napkin. "My mom is doing her volunteer work this afternoon, so I didn't know where to reach her to ask her what to do. I think it's her day to play checkers with Tex."

"And my mom has a meeting this afternoon. Dad's out of town on a job. We figured you were the next-best thing. Mrs. Lawrence told us you were here."

Amy glanced at her younger friend. "Laura insisted we come rather than call."

"I remembered what you said, Mrs. Parks," Laura told her. "I figured Katie would appreciate people sticking by her. It's going to be hard at school because, like, everyone's going to know."

She toyed with her cookie. "I don't know how Katie will take it, but I just wanted you to tell her for me she'll have at least one person standing by her tomorrow at school. Two, counting Amy."

"It's a wonderful gesture." Gracie told her warmly. "Even if Katie isn't able to acknowledge it right away, she'll appreciate the support. I'm sure of it."

Amy now added, "Laura and I had a long talk. She told me she'd talked to you. I had no idea she was feeling left out."

"I know. It was my problem," Laura said softly. She smiled at Amy.

Gracie was glad to see the strengthened bond between these two young friends. "Your gesture of friendship is lovely, really." She paused, debating how to handle the situation. Katie would probably be embarrassed, and she wasn't sure how her parents would react to the realization that the news was out.

"I don't expect the Nickolsons back for another hour or so, at the very least. How about I tell Katie that you stopped over and that you'll talk to her tomorrow in school?"

"Okay. We're going together to band practice." Laura smiled proudly.

Amy added, "I've been singing with them sometimes, and not just from the choir."

Gracie looked at her fondly.

"We want to give a great performance," Amy went on.

"It's for the Lord, after all, and Pastor Paul believes in us. We don't want to disappoint him—or God."

Gracie grinned. "God is always the perfect audience."

Amy smiled. "I'm really looking forward to the youth service. The whole idea is great. A lot of kids ask questions about God and stuff." She paused. "It's weird, Gracie. I like church, but my parents have been taking me practically since before I was born. Some other kids are different—they think it's . . . weird!"

"Well, you have the right idea," Gracie told her. "It's exciting to see youngsters who take their faith seriously. And you're the best kind of example—no one would ever think *you're* weird!"

Amy and Laura both giggled.

"Is Katie in big trouble?" Laura changed the subject now. "Will she go to jail?"

"No, she's not going to be put in jail," Gracie assured her. "But she is in big trouble. She went along with something illegal."

"Well, everybody makes mistakes," Amy reminded her. "Everyone does stupid things—things they wish they could fix or erase."

"Thankfully, they *can* be erased. But, often, not without a blemish. Our mistakes usually affect others, as well."

Gracie wanted them to understand that the truth was

sometimes as hard as it was liberating. She would not sugarcoat grace.

"We still have to live with the consequences of our mistakes. Katie's parents will have a hard time trusting her. And some other friends may judge her harshly. She might not be allowed to return to the mall for an extended period."

"And," Laura added, "she'll most likely be grounded by her parents—big time!"

Gracie looked serious. "Maybe. But it's small price to learn the lesson now. And, keep in mind that she's already been forgiven. Most likely her parents already have. Sure, they're mad at her, and disappointed. But they love her—she's their daughter."

Amy met her gaze. "And God, right? God has already forgiven her. He loves her, knowing full well all the mistakes she's going to make. Pastor Paul taught us that at youth group."

"Most assuredly by God," Gracie confirmed. "Our Lord believes in second chances—third, fourth—to the umpteenth."

"But I'm still going to pray for her." Laura was adamant.

"Prayer, for sure, is the most practical thing we can do," Gracie agreed.

"Sometimes, it's taken for granted," added Amy. "People may only try it when all else fails."

Gracie knew differently, just as her young friend did.

Prayer was the vanguard, unleashing the power of God to transform seemingly hopeless situations.

"Listen, girls," Gracie said. "I know you care about Katie, and it was wonderful having this surprise visit. Now, let me give each of you a hug!"

Gracie was curled up in the overstuffed recliner, cuddling Darren when his parents returned. She glanced at her watch: almost seven o'clock. If she hurried, she could join her household for chili or whatever else Marge had magicked out of her freezer.

Katie dashed by and bounded up the stairs, not even acknowledging Gracie's or her baby brother's presence. Darren sat disappointed, his arms still in the air.

Phyllis shot Gracie an apologetic look and picked up her son, while Terry issued an order to his stepdaughter to return and greet their guest and apologize for her rude behavior.

They heard the sound of a door slamming.

"She's embarrassed," Phyllis apologized for her daughter.

"So she should be!" Terry looked at Gracie. "I'm not going to apologize for her, Gracie. She's got to do that, herself, tomorrow, when she's in a better state of mind."

"But for now, thank you for staying with Darren," Phyllis said in a low voice. She looked on the verge of tears.

Gracie told them she'd loved having time alone with Darren and excused herself for a minute, to call home.

"Everything fine?" she asked when Marge answered.

"Nothing a few stitches didn't take care of," Marge said, matter-of-factly. She then explained that Rocky had gouged his palm when yanking on the satellite dish trying to readjust it.

"It was deeper than wide, so they used those butterfly clips. But then he put up a fight with the nurse when she suggested a tetanus shot. According to him, he didn't need one!" Marge chuckled. "The doc won, and poor Rocky went white as a sheet when the nurse got out the needle. I loved it!"

"I'll see you in a few minutes," she told Marge.

"Do you want to stay for supper, Gracie?" Phyllis asked as she hung up.

"That's very kind of you, but Marge has some ready at home."

Terry glanced up from his place on the floor next to the baby. "You really are okay? I know Darren can be a handful."

"We read, and I rocked him for a while. He serenaded me in that sweet little jabber, and I sang along. It was great to recall all those favorite lullabies."

Phyllis looked at Gracie sadly. "What are we going to do?" she said. It was clear she didn't really expect an answer.

Gracie walked over to put her arms around her, and Phyllis began to cry. "Katie's never done anything like this before! She says she didn't take anything—has never taken anything. I want to believe her—"

She pushed away to look at Gracie. "All those presents from Ashley—maybe they're not gifts."

"We have to believe her, honey." Terry's tone was consoling. "She's never lied to you before. When the chips are down, we've got to stand by our own."

Phyllis shook her head. "But Terry, Ashley says they *all* stole things. She claims it was a game—that the other girls put the items in her bag."

"And you believe her?" Terry pushed himself up. "That security guard said Katie drew the attention to the group. She actually blew the whistle on Ashley by protesting too loudly."

Phyllis shook her head. "I don't know what to believe."

"I'm inclined to think Katie did that on purpose, hoping to get caught. And after all, Jim Thompson was right outside the store. She almost said so herself, honey."

He put his arms around his wife. "Her behavior has been begging confrontation—and asking indirectly that we rein her in. I'm just sorry we didn't see this coming."

"It's all our fault." Phyllis was crying again.

Gracie felt like an intruder, but watched, pleased and yet surprised at Terry's support.

"But all those CDs, Terry! And the clothing, the makeup. She's got tons of that stuff in her room!"

As Terry soothed his wife, Gracie picked up her sweater

and began walking to the door. She intended to slip out before they noticed her taking her leave.

Phyllis saw her movements and called out, "Thanks for coming, Gracie!"

Gracie smiled. "I'd love to babysit again. I don't get enough time with my only grandchild. I adore spoiling your boy. You and Terry need to take Katie out. Talk to her."

Terry and Phyllis exchanged worried looks. "Maybe we could get a better handle on what's going on with her. What do you think, honey?" Terry asked his wife.

"Let's just get through this evening. In the morning, I'll be able to think more clearly."

Just then, just as she was about to shut the door, Gracie remembered to tell them about Amy's and Laura's visit. "Laura is just the kind of friend Katie needs right now."

Terry looked at his wife. "I don't want her with *those* girls. Any of them. But Gracie may be right, honey. Laura's a pretty straight kid—no angles to her. And she understands what it's like to have a stepparent. I think they'd be good for each other."

Phyllis set her lips. "We'll see about Laura. Katie's betrayed my trust. Something that's perhaps hard for you to understand."

Terry stared at his wife, his expression hard to read.

Then he said, "Of course, you're her mother. I leave it to you."

"She's an accomplice to a crime." Phyllis was firm.

Gracie could only wonder what was behind her stern reaction. But she knew that, even more than before, now it was time to leave.

12

GRACIE WHEELED THE GROCERY CART toward the cashier. "You're not handicapped, Rocky. You've just got stitches!"

"I don't see why I can't just eat at Abe's or at your place. Come on, Gracie, I hate shopping! I'm not going to eat this stuff anyway."

He scowled at her selection of fresh fruits, the healthy selection of frozen entrees, bread, and cereal. "I hate bean sprouts."

"I didn't buy any!" She grabbed a bottle of hydrogen peroxide and one of witch hazel. "I don't suppose you have these in the house either?"

"Nope," he replied. "Don't need them."

"Did you unwrap the wound, wash it and put antiseptic on it, like the doctor suggested?"

"Nope," he said again. "Didn't need to."

The man was infuriating! What had started out as a helpful excursion was turning out to be a fiasco. When Gracie had returned from the Nickolsons, they'd planned this trip over dinner.

"I'm only trying to be helpful! Is your porch fixture still burned out?" she asked, spying the light bulb display at the end of the aisle.

He gave an affirmative grunt. She picked up two packages.

"Hey, remember who's paying the bill here!"

She rolled her eyes. "Soap. Need any?"

He shook his head. "Gracie, I hereby release you from your imagined debt of gratitude for services not rendered."

"I feel *terrible* that you got hurt on my roof." She reached for the liquid detergent on the top shelf. "I'll do your laundry, but I need some more of this."

Rocky stepped in her way. "Here let me get it. Like you said, I'm not handicapped." He struggled to grab the handle of the container with his left hand, but when he pulled it off the shelf, it slipped and came down with a loud *thud* on his foot.

"Great balls of fire, woman!" He hopped, holding the opposite foot, waving his wounded hand in the air. "My foot's broken!"

The plastic had split on impact and Rocky was dancing in a puddle of blue goo. Gracie grabbed his elbow, trying to remain focused as her companion emitted every sound of pain he could think of.

In a few minutes the stock boy had come to their rescue, but then he managed to slip in the detergent. He grabbed Rocky's bad arm to keep from falling, and sent both men back against the shelf full of paper towels, which, of course, came tumbling down around them.

Uncle Miltie turned the aisle just in time to get hit in the stomach with a roll Rocky had kicked into the air. "This isn't a football field, Gravino! And that's about the *worst* punt I've ever seen!"

"There's nothing funny about this!" Rocky shouted as Uncle Miltie began to chuckle.

He was right, but Gracie was still laughing as they got into the check-out line.

Gracie wiped her eyes and started putting the items on the conveyor belt. The woman in front of her turned and stared, her face disapproving.

Darla Knight. Gracie recognized Ashley's mother. The woman gave a stiff smile and turned back to the cashier, just as Uncle Miltie rejoined them with his arms full.

He plunked down two cans of Spam, a box of crackers and a large bag of gingersnaps. He grinned happily. "Emergency staples."

Darla was looking at them again, so he explained, "Never

know when Gracie's going to get called off somewhere. Last night, it was baby-sitting for the Nickolsons. Tomorrow it might be a trip to the Big Apple to see her grandson." He smiled at Gracie. "I know you, it's only a matter of weeks until you're planning a trip to visit Arlen. And the way you've been going on and on about how cute Darren Nickolson is, it just might be tomorrow! And I want to be prepared!"

"Is there something wrong at the Nickolsons'?" Darla wanted to know.

Gracie was not sure what to say. "They're looking to find ways to spend more time with Katie . . . getting a new sibling is never easy, particularly in her situation."

Darla's mouth twisted, and, holding her credit card, she turned back to the girl at the register.

"Declined, ma'am. Do you have another form of payment?"

"That one's perfectly good!" Darla told the teenager. "The problem must be *your* machine."

The girl apologized. "I could call my boss—"

"It won't be necessary. I'm in a hurry." Darla plunked down another credit card. "Just be sure to get this register checked!"

Uncle Miltie shot Gracie a "What gives with her?" look.

Rocky ventured, "The planet doesn't revolve fast enough for some of us, I guess."

Darla must have heard, because she turned around and

smiled more convincingly. "Computers! They're always screwing things up. There's *plenty* of money in that account, so I really don't understand it."

She picked up her bag. "Give my best to Phyllis. Tell her I'm sorry she can't make the investment group tonight. We'll all miss her."

Gracie took the opportunity to ask, "Is Jess going? Her kids have been sick."

Darla switched her bag to the other hip. "It's just for us original members, or at least the ones who were already in place. The old crowd, you might say." She headed for the exit.

Uncle Miltie watched her leave. "Something about her bothers me—"

"Or something's missing," Rocky said. "Like a personality."

Gracie eyed her uncle and their friend. "Remember the cream filling."

"You need something else, Gracie?" Rosie the cashier was getting impatient. "Cream filling's over there."

Gracie laughed. "Old family saying."

"Huh?"

Gracie explained.

"I don't know about any filling," Rosie said. "But Mrs. Knight's crusty enough. This isn't the first time she's had trouble with her credit cards."

Gracie decided to think more about that unexpected piece of information later.

"Let's try to give each other the benefit of the doubt," Gracie said, glancing between her men. "We all have off days."

"Some of us more off than on." Uncle Miltie was watching Darla through the plate window. "She sure cuts a classy appearance, though."

"Only goes to prove," Rocky said, "that appearances certainly *can* be deceiving."

Gracie hated to admit the truth in that, but she would pray to see the best even in Darla Knight. Right now, she was more concerned with Jess and what further problems might be brewing at the meeting that was excluding her friend. She made a mental note to pay a visit to the Horton household.

Abe's Delicatessen was one of the most popular places in town, luring customers from the street with the scent of potato kugel and warm pastries. Stopping there seemed to be the perfect pick-me-up after what had become a thoroughly exhausting morning. Gracie graciously allowed Rocky to pull open the door with his good hand. He waved her in, with a mock flourish.

He was still limping, though Gracie wasn't sure if he hadn't merely developed it for effect. Rocky did love attention, as much as he grumbled he didn't. She smiled at him and clucked sympathetically.

"Come on, fellow," Uncle Miltie said, stepping around him. "Don't let an old man beat you to a seat next to a pretty lady."

Abe Wasserman knew as much about his customers as any priest or doctor. And Gracie knew it was as much Abe's comforting welcome as the savor of his cuisine that put people at ease enough to confide in him.

Jim Thompson showed up just after Gracie had exchanged family news with Abe, who'd talked to his sister Sophie the night before. She put down the menu. "I don't know why I bother to read this, anyway," she told them. "Nothing competes with the curative powers of Abe's chicken noodle soup."

"I'll take a bowl of that, too," said Jim Thompson.

"Grilled Reuben—heavy on the dressing, light on the sauerkraut," said Rocky.

"Lentil soup for me," said Uncle Miltie. "And a buttered roll."

Jim now turned to study Rocky. "So, what happened? Shoud I worry about the other guy?"

"*Hmmph!*" Uncle Miltie acknowledged. "Truth is, this *fool* here was trying to use his fingers as if they were pliers."

Rocky scowled. "Because *this* fool bought a defective satellite dish on sale. Cheap thing had ragged edges."

Gracie looked stern. "Stop!"

"Enough with the *Grumpy Old Men* routine," Abe told him. "It doesn't look good on either of us, Gravino. We Italians are known for our spirit."

Jim wrinkled his face. "Wasserman?"

"On my mother's side," Abe told him. "Italian Jews."

Jim made an impressed look. "So, that's the secret! What we have here is part deli, part trattoria—a sort of pasta parlor with extra pizazz, hold the anchovies. . . ."

"Well, I've never heard of a pastrami pizza," Uncle Miltie scoffed.

"Gracie," Abe said, changing the subject, "do you know anything about these kids shoplifting?" He glanced at Jim and quickly realized that he might have said the wrong thing.

Jim shot Gracie a furtive look. "Whole town seems to know. I wish folks were as quick to praise as they are to pass on bad news."

"I'm not just gossiping. I *know* these girls and their families, and when something like that happens in Willow Bend, it concerns all of us. Because we care."

Gracie started to say something, but Jim began speaking first. "I don't think it's right for me to comment. But I'm involved not just because I'm an officer of the law but because, as you say, Abe, I *care*."

Gracie now asked Rocky if Jess had come back to work yet.

"No, she hasn't," he said carefully. "The kids are still sick, I think."

"I plan to visit them today," Gracie told him.

"There was a fellow in here asking about her," Abe told them. "Sort of important looking. I sent him right to the newspaper office."

"Are you certain it wasn't self-importance?" Uncle Miltie asked, with a little chuckle.

Rocky stopped mid-bite. "Hey! He dropped by our office, I know—but he didn't give his name. I don't know where he went after he found out Jess wasn't at her desk."

Could it have been the man she saw the day she and Laura were picking up apples, Gracie wondered. "Did he tell you anything, Abe?"

Abe shrugged. "Nope. But I can tell you, he's not from around here," Abe concluded. "He had bit of an accent—New Jersey, maybe. Said he'd had a long drive, is all."

Gracie was curious. "Nothing else?"

"When I asked him what brought him to Willow Bend, he wasn't forthcoming. 'Business' was his only answer."

Abe ended his story with "I let it go at that. I might know almost everybody's business, but I don't pry."

"Well, if he comes in again, how about breaking your rule?" Rocky said. "I'm curious about any fellow who might be harassing my employees."

Abe furrowed his brow. "How's that?"

"It's just a hunch I have." Rocky was cagey. "Something's going on with my new editor. And I think that fellow might be it."

Since they needed time to talk, Gracie was glad the children weren't home when she arrived at the Hortons's place.

Bobby was on an afterschool field trip, and Molly had gone to the home of a friend from preschool for the afternoon. Jess, however, still seemed distracted.

Gracie opened the tin of double-chocolate brownies she'd baked for the family, while Jess made tea. They engaged in small talk, both careful to avoid problematic subjects.

They sat across from each other at the kitchen table without saying anything until Gracie decided to break the silence.

"Rocky's worried about you."

"I explained things to him the best I could."

Gracie plowed on. "And I talked to Marilyn. She was concerned, as well."

"Did she tell you that Darla thinks I took the money?"

"No, she didn't."

"Well, Darla implied as much to everyone in the group—Marilyn told me."

The situation was making Gracie a little more than uncomfortable. Gracie hated gossip. Not unlike her brownies, gossip could be delicious—and bad for you, at the same time.

"Marilyn told you about the special board meeting?"

Jess nodded. "She called me last night, right after they met. Darla wants to ask me to leave the group. They're going to absorb the loss for the sake of *friendship*.

"But, Gracie, I tell you, I did *not* take that money!" Jess burst into tears. "And R. J. was *not* an embezzler! It's so crazy! Everything's just so out of control!"

Gracie looked at her sympathetically as Jess began to spill out the whole story. Her husband has been the creative force in his working partnership. At one point he had developed a special digital technique for reading old manuscripts, and a man named Walter Blackstock had given him some venture capital.

But then, unfortunately, another researcher had beaten R. J. to the patent, and Blackstock lost his money. But he was a shrewd businessman and continued to bank on his partner's scientific creativity. The investment looked to be paying off, but then R. J. got sick. He died while they were still working on a prototype, and his mentor, Dr. Simmons, had no deal with Blackstock.

"Walter was really mad," Jess went on. "But there was nothing I could do. For the sake of the college, and taking his own interests into account, Carroll Simmons wouldn't cooperate. He has every right to protect his work. There was nothing wrong with that!"

"I don't understand the accusation—embezzlement?"

Jess dabbed her eyes. "Walter was out a lot of money. This came to a head right after R. J. died. I thought it was over. There was nothing I could do to secure a patent on my husband's ideas. I thought Walter had dropped it. But it seems he blamed R. J. and accused him of embezzling money to cover up his own shortfall.

"Walter used the money from one project to invest in

another. That's the way venture capitalism works. The problem is, the investment didn't live to realize the profit," Jess said sadly. She added, "So Blackstock was stuck."

"I guess he figured your husband wasn't around to fight back."

"Or tell his own side of the story. I talked to Dr. Simmons, and he assures me R. J.'s innovations are marketable, but it's just that the bugs are still a long way from being worked out.

"Gracie, I trust him. He's promised to give R. J. credit and register a patent on my behalf—but only when the time is right. But right now, R. J. is accused of being a thief. And I don't have the money to clear his name!"

Gracie looked at Jess. Her expression was determined. "My dear, I intend to help you in any way I can."

She didn't add that, at the moment, Jess was suspected of being a thief, as well.

PHYLLIS HAD OBVIOUSLY been crying again. Gracie searched her mind for the right words, but it was Darren who brought comfort, calling out, "Mama!"

He extended his arms from the playpen, hopping and squealing.

"I'll get him," Gracie offered.

Phyllis thanked her. "No, I think he needs to be changed. I can do that before we leave."

"Where's Terry?" Gracie asked, glancing around the quiet house. Phyllis let a cloud of worry cross her face before answering.

"He's meeting someone for lunch. I've left you the restaurant number."

Gracie nodded. "And Katie?"

"Outside, I guess. She's grounded for the time being."

Gracie studied her friend. Phyllis was clearly upset with her husband, but there was no point in prying. Gracie knew the best thing for her to do was simply to offer the support she was already giving.

"I'll change him." Phyllis put Darren on the telephone stand that served as a makeshift dressing table next to the crib.

"Katie and Darren have already had lunch. You can give him a bottle and put him down for a nap. We'll probably be back before he gets up. I have to work tonight."

Gracie moved beside her, smiling at Darren, and offering her finger to his outstretched hands. "Are you going to sing to me today?" She cooed at him.

As she played with her baby, Phyllis noticeably relaxed. "Gracie, we need your prayers," she confessed softly. "Terry and I have been fighting over how to handle this. There just aren't any easy answers...."

"There never are," Gracie told her. "And I know you know that. But you also know God loves Katie. He wants the best for her. It hurts Him when His children sin, just as no parent wants his or her child to suffer."

Phyllis sighed heavily. "I feel like I'm a failure as a mother—and wife."

"I don't believe that."

"I didn't want a divorce. I knew it would hurt Katie. But her father insisted. Now he lives in California—where, I don't know. He hasn't contacted her in over a year. She blames Terry for that, too.

"Terry and Darren are the best things to happen to me

since Katie. But juggling a new marriage, a baby and an almost adolescent's problems . . . oh, it's making me crazy!"

Gracie motioned for them to sit down, and chose the rocking chair next to Darren's pile of books and toys.

"Terry loves Katie. Gracie, he's trying so hard. But he's never been married before. He doesn't have the same sense of priorities as I do. He can't see that we have to be the models for what we expect for our children. And we need to be tough when they disobey."

As Gracie rocked, she reached out to take Darren.

"After you left the other night, we went up to talk to Katie." Phyllis now said, leaning back in her chair and closing her eyes. "It's funny, Terry can be so reasonable. He's the better parent, really. He's more of her advocate than Katie will ever realize. He coaxed the story out of her.

"She told us that a loud quarrel between the girls was what apparently tipped off store security. Katie says Ashley put the CD in her backpack so that she couldn't claim she didn't take anything."

Phyllis sighed again. "It really scared Katie. Thank goodness, Jim Thompson was there. He helped the store owner see reason. But now, all of a sudden, Ashley's telling kids that Katie framed *her*. Poor Katie isn't popular enough, really, to have anyone rally to her defense. They're all scared of Ashley, anyway."

Gracie looked thoughtful as she heard this.

"So I grounded Katie until further notice. Terry didn't agree, but he never goes against me. It seemed a way to protect her, as much as a punishment, I thought.

"Today, she came home from school early. That's why I called you. She had a show-down with Ashley. Laura Clayton was there and tried to help, but the principal gave both girls a three-day, out-of-school suspension.

"Terry came home early to help me handle the problem. He was mad at me—I think he secretly blames me for her behavior, and yet Katie was wrong about which of us had taken her side. Terry and I started arguing, and then Katie got in it. Terry brought up the fact that Laura had come by to offer her friendship the other evening but that I'd held back, when you told me. I never told her, you see, so Katie decided she didn't believe him, and called him a liar. I was dumbstruck. I should have said something—I couldn't."

Gracie lifted a sleepy Darren to her shoulder and rocked him as Phyllis went on with her story.

Katie accused them both of meddling in her life. She blamed their marriage for her father's lack of attention to her and Terry's self-indulgent spending as the reason she couldn't have what the other kids did.

"Terry took it all straight on," Phyllis told. "I could see him tremble with anger. He never said a word in his own defense, Gracie. I felt so awful. She hurt him—a lot. I stood there and

let her. Then Katie demanded he leave. And he did just that."
Phyllis looked at Gracie. "I've ruined a second marriage."

"No, you didn't." Gracie met her gaze. "You're having lunch with him today."

"I only hope it's not to say good-bye. I called him at work. I knew he took the day off, but I figured that was where he'd go."

Gracie snuggled Darren, lifting his soft flannel blanket to cover his shoulders. The baby was sleeping. She closed her eyes and opened her heart to God. She wasn't a marriage counselor, or even a pastor, but this family needed her.

Father, put Your love around them. This afternoon, give them the respite they need. Help them to see each other afresh, in this time of mistrust and conflict. Help them to find solutions where it now seems there aren't any.

"Gracie," Phyllis said, softly. "Is Darren asleep?"

She nodded. "I sometimes feel rocking a baby is the closest we come to experiencing heaven here on earth—even if Uncle Miltie claims living in Willow Bend is!"

"I agree with you!" Phyllis looked strengthened by their discussion and by Gracie's prayers. "I'm going go meet Terry now."

"I'll keep on praying," Gracie said. "And you do the same."

Phyllis stood up to go. "Of course, I will, Gracie dear. Now I'll check on Katie. I think she's out in her treehouse. She goes there when she's unhappy, or at odds with the world. I'm glad she has such a refuge, even when she uses it to get away from me!"

After Phyllis left, Gracie put Darren to bed and went to look for Katie. She strolled around the yard, admiring the small tidy vegetable garden.

"Mrs. Parks—up here!"

The voice came from the window of a white clapboard treehouse with red shutters. A box of blue petunias framed the deck. Katie stood there, waving at her. "Can you come up?"

Gracie glanced up. The ladder didn't look too intimidating, but the door was a bit small. "I'll try." She climbed up, squeezed in and sat on the pile of pillows across from Katie.

"I feel just horrible," Katie said. "I can't do *anything* right! Now my parents will get a divorce, and Mom's going to have another nervous breakdown! It's all my fault!"

Gracie reassured her. "They're not going to get divorced."

"Are you sure? I said some awful things. They yelled at each other. I don't think they love each other anymore."

"They do. If they didn't love each other and you, that wouldn't be the case, and the upset would feel different, believe me. They're trying to find their way as a couple and as parents. That isn't always easy."

"Well, me getting into trouble can't help! I knew some day Ashley would get caught! I should have known better than to hang around with her."

Katie's face was a study in misery. Gracie wanted to hug her but also knew it was best to proceed cautiously. She watched the girl struggling with her conscience and with regrets.

"You probably hate me," Katie said abruptly.

"Of course not!"

"You should. I hate myself."

Gracie met her gaze. "We all make mistakes, Katie. The important thing is that we learn from them. And something like this is never going to happen again, is it?"

"Never! I'm never going to be that stupid again!" Katie looked resolute. And Gracie had to suppress a smile at her fervor.

"They told me that I couldn't see Ashley. What they didn't ask is whether I wanted to or not. I hate Ashley! She used me to get good grades in math and always wanted to boss me around. Besides, even if I did want to see her, she doesn't want to see me."

Gracie waited for her to explain.

"If I hadn't given us away in the shop, they wouldn't have gotten caught. There's good reason to hate me."

"Or *thank* you."

Katie shook her head. "It doesn't work that way."

Gracie reasoned with her. "Katie, dear, it appears like that right now, but there'll come a day when Ashley realizes you did the right thing. Deep down, she knows even now that you were right."

"No, she doesn't! She says she tells everybody that she hates me! That I'm the one that framed her!"

Katie paused to think. She went on seriously, "Life has gotten so complicated. It seems like only yesterday Terry was dating my mom. He built me this house, you know. He and his dad."

"I didn't know."

"Grandpas are cool. Mom's dad came over to help Art and Terry."

Gracie felt a twinge of regret. El would have been a good grandfather.

"Mrs. Parks, it's just natural to love your real kids more than the adopted ones, isn't it?"

Gracie didn't know how to answer.

"I mean, it's unrealistic to believe Terry loves me as much as Darren. I'm not his *real* daughter. They're just kidding themselves—but they're not fooling me."

Gracie now slipped her arm around Katie's shoulders and pulled her close.

"You feel real to me," Gracie soothed her.

Katie relaxed in Gracie's embrace. "That's not what I mean. I'm not his flesh and blood, like Darren."

"But you're the child of his heart—he chose you."

Katie gritted her teeth. "He chose my mom."

"It was a package deal, Katie. He understood that going into the relationship. Don't you think they struggled with the decision to marry? Your mother had been hurt terribly. Terry had never been married. They took a risk. Believe me, they love you, and each other very much."

Katie said only, *"Hmmm."*

Gracie looked into her young friend's eyes. "And don't you know he can love more than one person! *You* do, you told me yourself. You love two grandfathers, and probably grandmothers, as well."

Katie nodded.

"And Darren."

"Most of the time." She grinned. "No, I'm just kidding—he's the best thing that has happened to our family."

Gracie squeezed Katie's shoulders. "Speaking of Darren, I'd better go back and check on him."

Katie flashed a smile much like her mother's. "He sleeps all afternoon. Mom calls it her 'blessed rest.'"

"I can see you love her, too."

"Of course!"

"We can love lots of people, can't we?"

"Yeah." The corners of her mouth turned up, revealing dimples. "Thanks, Mrs. Parks. I guess I do love Terry."

"He loves you, too."

Katie climbed down ahead of Gracie and helped her to the ground. They were walking toward the house when Katie stopped short of the threshold. "I've disappointed them terribly. They'll never trust me again."

"Of course they will." Gracie put her arm around the girl again. "They haven't given up hope."

"Mrs. Parks, what should I do?"

Gracie laughed. "Have a snack with me. Everything looks better after cookies and nice cool milk!"

They crossed the threshold arm in arm.

Gracie peeked in on Darren, who was sleeping soundly, sucking on his fingers. When she got to the kitchen, Katie had opened a bag of graham crackers and filled their glasses.

"I'll bet you're a big help to your mother."

Katie shook her head. "Doesn't she wish! I'm a brat, really. Spoiled rotten. Mom's been giving in to me since the day my dad left. No, the truth is, I help when I feel like it—when I want something. There's a lot of things about myself I'm not proud of. But how do I begin again?"

"I think you already have. Your parents are behind you. They're concerned, of course, but they're on your team."

Katie nodded. "I'm scared."

"Lord," Gracie began, reaching for Katie's hand, "fill this child with grace. Show her clearly Your forgiveness. Strengthen her resolve to live in Your light."

Gracie's cell phone rang.

"Aren't you going to get it?" Katie asked. "It might be important."

Gracie hated to break the healing mood of the moment,

but glancing at the number, she recognized the caller as Amy Cantrell.

"Gracie, my car won't start. I think it's the battery, but I can't tell for sure. I'm sitting at school, in the parking lot, waiting for my dad. The thing is, I'm suppose to pick Laura up at four, to take her to the library to work on a report. Her mom took Patsy for physical therapy."

Gracie relayed the information. "Amy's father is on the way, but Laura Clayton needs a ride home from the Mid-County Rec Center and Amy was going to bring her. She doesn't know how long it's going to take to fix her car, so Amy wonders if I can do it."

"I wouldn't mind riding along," Katie said timidly.

Gracie remembered Darren. She glanced at her watch. It was almost three. Phyllis had promised to be home by three. She explained the problem to Amy, who said her father would get Laura if Gracie couldn't.

"Thanks tons, anyway!" Amy said. "My dad's here now. Maybe we won't need you. I'll call you back."

Gracie flipped the phone closed and slid it back in her pocket. "Well, we wait."

"For my parents?"

"And to see if Amy's father can get that old jalopy of hers running."

"It'll be good to get out of the house," Katie said.

Gracie cautioned, "You'll have to okay going with your parents."

"Well, that blows that idea! Terry won't let me go anywhere."

"I think that was your mom's decision. They might see things differently, considering you're going with me and we're picking up Laura."

Katie was not so convinced.

Phyllis and Terry returned less than ten minutes later. Not surprisingly, their conversation with Katie was strained—things weren't going to be better overnight—but they were open to her going to pick up Laura with Gracie, if Amy couldn't.

Gracie's phone now rang again. She listened for a second.

"We're off!" she said to Phyllis and Terry, giving them each a quick hug.

"Bye, Mom! Bye, Dad!" Katie said. And then, under her breath: "I love you." She followed Gracie out the door.

JESS WAS IN THE CLAYTON KITCHEN when Gracie returned from the library with Laura and Katie. Bobby and Molly were playing in the yard just within eyesight of the kitchen window.

"They've gotten over the worst of the chicken pox, I see," Gracie said. She watched Bobby push his sister on the swing. "They seem to be getting along rather well, too, and after such a long confinement."

She turned to Jess. "Now that's success!"

"Molly's got a small scar on her chin," Jess pointed out. "She couldn't help picking at the scab. And as far as their getting along, I think there's truth to the saying that what doesn't kill a kid makes him sweeter . . . for a few days, anyway."

Gracie laughed. "I don't know that one."

"They were both so miserable, the only thing that made

them feel better was being with each other. Misery loves company! They curled up on the couch and colored or watched TV. It was actually quality time. I took time off work, and we were all home together."

Gracie wondered if she dared address the problem of the editor's absences from the newspaper, but it was Jess who brought up the subject. "The paper's been very accommodating."

She looked at Gracie. "In fact they've been so accommodating, I've taken advantage of them." Her smile was tinged with unease. "I hope I have a job to go back to."

"Rocky is fair," Gracie told her. "But was it just the children's illness that's kept you away from work? He was worried about you."

Jess pulled her shoulders in. "I'm not a fighter, Gracie. When attacked, I run for cover. Blackstock wants me to sign a paper giving him rights to any patent Carroll might register in R. J.'s name having to do with the project he invested in.

"Now he's hounding me. Marilyn thinks I should issue a restraining order, but I'm not sure if I want to drag the police into this. I've been hoping he'd just go away—along with the problems with the investment group. I haven't done anything wrong! Why is this happening to me?"

"I know I don't have to tell you that the best thing to do with any problem is to confront it," Gracie offered. "That's where strength abides. And without those folks who are willing to be brave and face up to things, the rest of us wouldn't have role models." Gracie smiled encouragingly. "I know it may not seem like enough. But that's the reality of life—we don't get all the answers."

"Life's a mystery," Jess agreed. But she sounded defeated before she'd even begun.

"Just because God keeps life mysterious," Gracie told her, sharing one of her favorite rules, "that doesn't mean you should ever stop trying to solve the mystery." She glanced over at Marilyn, who'd been listening quietly. "Now, what do you say we get to the bottom of one of them? I think our thief is feeling pretty vulnerable right now, and with a little bit of love, we might just get a confession!"

Jess stared, dumbfounded. "You know who did it?"

"I think, deep down, we all three do."

Marilyn nodded. "I dislike feeling that Ashley's behavior is a matter of the apple falling noticeably close to the tree . . . but. . . ." She shrugged.

Gracie looked at her. "I'd be surprised if God weren't working this out in ways only He can see."

"But six hundred dollars! That's *pin* money to Darla! Ashley practically spends that much on some of her shopping excursions!" Jess was unconvinced.

Gracie now posed the question: "What if Darla considered it a loan? Maybe she was planning to put it back, but in the meantime, you volunteered to be treasurer?"

"But why?" Jess still looked doubtful. "She doesn't need money."

Gracie nodded. "So it appears. I haven't figured the reason out, but I intend to."

"Here's my news," Marilyn said, changing the subject slightly. "I've turned in my resignation to the Kidnappers."

"What?" Jess stared her friend. "When did you do that?"

Marilyn glanced out the window. "Yesterday, when we met. We were all too quick to jump to conclusions—to cast blame. And I just decided I had other priorities."

Marilyn smiled at Jess. "As much as I'd like to say I did it in solidarity with you, I did it as much for myself. And really, Jess, *nobody* wanted to believe it was you."

Jess nodded her appreciation. "So, what do we do next?"

"Pray for Darla, Ashley and her father," Gracie told them.

Don Delano handed Gracie a cup of tea at the Ecumenical Luncheon. "I love these affairs! They should have them more than a couple of times a year. What nicer way to spend an afternoon? Good music, an inspiring speaker—and, of course, great catering by Gracie and company!"

Gracie accepted the compliment. "Speaking of which, where's Marge?"

"I haven't seen her," Don said, looking around. "Maybe she got stuck at the store."

"No, she actually closed up to help me. She was here before, during the setup, I just haven't seen her since." Gracie scanned the room one more time. "Oh, well, she's around somewhere."

"By the way," Don said, changing the subject, "what's with your intention to talk to Darla Knight?"

Gracie said, "Paul and I are going over there later today. She has a house to show this afternoon."

"It must be the place across the street from Claytons'— some rich guy is interested in investment property," Don told her.

"Some rich guy?"

"That's what Ashley says. Darla's hoping to sell him a few of Willow Bend's less desirable parcels for rentals. That place across from Claytons' is in sad shape, but so was that bungalow of the pastor's when he bought the place. It's the same vintage, so it has potential. I'd say it's a good investment."

Could it be just a coincidence that the property was across the street from Jess Horton? It might be time to tell Rocky what was going on, to share her concern—he'd know what to do.

"Ashley came in to see me, by the way, the day after she got in trouble. That's how I know this. She actually seemed quite contrite. She admitted to me that Katie had been helping with her homework assignments. Since that won't be true anymore, it was probably in her best interest to come clean, but I sensed some honest soul-searching."

"That's a first step," Gracie told him gratefully. "At least it's putting this lost lamb back on the path to the fold."

GRACIE ALWAYS ENJOYED visiting Rocky at his office. The *Mason County Gazette* office had character, from the tips of its dowdy, Depression-era ceiling fans to the well-worn seats of the oak swivel chairs.

The nostalgic atmosphere was helped by the "Loose Lips Sink Ships!" poster from World War II on the wall. An Underwood manual typewriter sat on the lefthand extension of Rocky's rolltop desk, with a computer on the other. Nearby, cacti in successive stages of expiration waited to die.

The staff greeted Gracie as the old friend she was. Ben Tomlinson and Mike Struthers both waved, while Sue Jameson smiled from where she sat, across from an empty desk with a little plaque on it that read "Jess Horton."

"Gracie!" Rocky called, hobbling out from the small, cluttered cubicle they called the break room. Even the stale black coffee smell it sent forth added to the place's atmosphere.

"How's the foot?" She noticed he was wearing a slipper, thanks to his unexpected date with the detergent.

He wiggled his toes. "Bruised, but not broken. Cup of coffee?" He lifted his mug.

She shook her head. "That stuff could take the tarnish off a spoon."

"Then what brings *you* here, if not our liquid hospitality?" he said, preceding her into his office. Gracie moved a pile of books to sit down.

Rover and Gent smiled out from a frame on the top of the editor's desk. Her pal was more attached to his basset hound and cocker than he'd care to admit. She scanned the sepia portraits of Mama and Papa and Grandpapa Gravino. There was an old photograph of him with her husband, holding a prize catch. "That seems like ages ago," she said, picking up the photograph.

"I guess it was. Lewes, Delaware, 1985. Biggest bluefish in the bay. El really won the lottery that trip."

Gracie nodded. "That was the year you went back East. Your mom got sick. You stayed in Philadelphia until she passed on. I remember."

"We go back a long way, don't we?"

She nodded, and returned the snapshot to its spot. There was also one of her and Marge, decked out in leis and floral shirts at the local AARP Hawaiian Night. And a photograph of Arlen and Wendy on their wedding day. She picked up the small one of her with little Elmo. She'd sent that to Rocky from New York City when she visited her son and his family a few months back.

"As I've told you before, you're really pretty sentimental, for such a hard-boiled guy."

"Like to keep my loved ones close."

So did Gracie. They regarded each other affectionately.

"So what do need, Gracie? You don't just pop in."

"That investor guy—from Jess's past—the one who once had the deal with her husband—did you know he's bothering Jess?"

"I suspected as much." He leaned back in his chair. "She hasn't talked to me about it yet. Probably she's embarrassed."

Gracie nodded. "She's afraid of him, I think. Now, he's looking at the property across the street from her house—at least I think it's him. That's why I came. I thought you could check it out. Maybe put a little pressure on the man to leave town."

"How do you know all this?"

She recounted the meeting with Don, and with Jess herself. She told him about seeing the man on Jess's porch. "He can't really make her sign over that patent, can he?"

"I don't know much about how they work. But I can have someone call the U.S. Patent Office and find out."

Gracie smiled. She'd brought the problem to the right place.

"How's the melodrama with the teenage kids caught shoplifting going? You still baby-sitting?"

She corrected him. "It's *not* a melodrama. They're real people, with real lives. I feel sorry for them. And I love spending time with babies. You know that!"

"Jim says that formal charges have been lodged against the one girl. They've banned her from the mall."

Gracie sighed. "I hope not by herself."

"You know, Gracie," he said, "Jim told me the mother didn't pick the girl up until half past eight. The father refused to drive here and get involved. Poor kid."

"I know," Gracie sighed.

"I think Darla Knight may be the culprit in the Kidnappers caper," Gracie told him. "I can't prove anything, but I'm hoping she'll confess."

Rocky laughed. "I know—you've been praying for her."

"How did you guess?"

Her friend just grinned at her affectionately.

"You use that antiseptic?"

A scowl. "We're not going there, Gracie."

"You're incorrigible."

He laughed. "Can I take you out to lunch?"

"I've got a lot of errands to run, because later this afternoon I'm meeting Paul. We're going to go over to the Knights's."

"Then the confession's a done deal. You two will call in the big guns—the heavenly ones. Darla doesn't stand a chance."

Gracie glanced at Jess Horton's empty desk. "Did she phone in sick again?"

"Oh no, your pastor picked her up for an early lunch about an hour ago."

Gracie's grin suddenly got wide. Her eyes blinked shut for an instant.

"Earth to Gracie!"

"I was praying," she explained. "A *different* sort of prayer."

"I suppose God loves all matchmakers. Then again, He might feel you were muscling in on His territory!"

Darla turned out not to be at home when Gracie and Paul stopped by. Ashley reluctantly let them in. She ushered them into a living room that had hardly a comfortable place to sit. Gracie and Paul settled themselves on the edge of a narrow white leather sofa. It squeaked unpleasantly under their combined weight.

"Perhaps we got the time wrong? I thought your mother said three-thirty this afternoon," Paul said to Ashley.

She shrugged. "She left in a hurry—she had to wrap up a deal, she said. She knew you were coming."

"Do you think she's coming back soon?" Paul asked.

"She didn't say." Ashley looked sulky.

Paul glanced at Gracie.

"I brought a little something." Gracie handed over a loaf of banana bread tied with a plaid ribbon and a jar of apple butter.

Ashley lowered her gaze. "You're friends with Katie's family." She was looking at Paul.

"I'd like to be with yours, as well."

She looked up. "My mom says she'd go to church if she had time. You know we've come sometimes. "

Gracie broke in, glancing at Paul first. "Your participation with the band has been great! I know you're busy, too. . ."

Ashley blinked quickly. Did Gracie detect tears? The girl stood up.

"I'll just put this in the kitchen. Would you all like a cup of tea? Or some juice? If you wait, I'll call my mom on her cell phone."

"I'd love some tea," Gracie replied. "Can I help?"

Ashley shook her head. "I only have to put on some water."

"Why don't I do that while you make that call?"

"Okay." Ashley gave them a shy grin. "I'll phone now! Be right back!"

Paul pointed to the wall. "But there's a phone right there."

"I have to use the bathroom." Ashley darted off.

Gracie raised her eyebrows. "What do you suppose that's all about?"

"I haven't the foggiest." He toyed with a bouquet of red silk poppies sitting in a vase at the center of the table. "I get the feeling this is a lonely house."

"Me, too."

"Darla did sound suspicious when I called. But when I told her how pleased we were to have Ashley and the band performing with the choir, and how talented she was, it seemed to put her somewhat more at her ease." He looked at Gracie. "Like you put Ashley at ease when you handed her that gift. I'm thinking they've been hurt, Gracie. Perhaps all this is merely defensive behavior."

Gracie glanced around. There were no photographs, books, or personal items. Nothing to give a clue as to who really lived in this expensive house. There were art books and expensive interior-decorating magazines, artfully arranged on the coffee table in the living room. But not one backpack plopped on the counter, or a sweater draped over a chair, to indicate the presence of a child.

"My mom's on her way," Ashley announced, standing in the doorway.

Ten minutes later Darla arrived. Gracie suspected she might have been there all along. She could barely sit still a moment before hopping up for sugar cubes instead of granular, candies she'd purchased in France, embroidered napkins bought on a trip to Italy.

Ashley, on the other hand, sat quietly, nibbling a chocolate-coated cookie. "Pastor Paul," she asked softly. "Do you really think we're okay? I mean, for church—not just for Quasi or Cedric's basement?" She lowered her gaze.

"I don't even have a Bible. It seems . . . I don't know, weird."

"I think," Paul said carefully, "your band is bringing us just the music we all need to hear. Plus, the choir seems to enjoy making it with you, and that's a real mark of approval."

Ashley gave a shy smile. Her mother watched the conversation and seemed at one moment about to say something but then set her lips.

"You're always welcome at the youth group," Paul now told the teenager. "I know you have a lot of friends and a busy schedule, but making time for it might turn out to surprise you—you'd know most of the other kids there, and I know they find it rewarding, because they tell me so."

"That's what I've heard," Ashley replied, glancing at her mother. "You're right, they wouldn't bother lying to you. What would be the point?"

Gracie, observing this exchange with her keen sense of empathy, understood that Ashley was a young woman caught in a very predictable kind of conflict: Torn between feeling cool and feeling good about herself, she looked to her mother for guidance and, unfortunately, encountered another soul in similar conflict.

The apple *didn't* fall far from the tree but, in this case, there was a Great Harvester at the ready. Or, at least, His emissary. Pastor Paul had managed already to engage Ashley and her bandmates in the joyful proceedings at Eternal Hope; now, here on this visit, he was pointing the way to a deeper involvement.

For both the girl and her mother.

Darla looked uncertain. "Ashley dear, would you *like* to try the youth group?"

"Only if you'll come and hear us at Eternal Hope, instead of always making excuses that you've got too much else to do."

Gracie smiled at Paul as she heard Darla answer, "It's a deal."

16

MARGE WALKED into Gracie's kitchen with unexpected tidings. Chad, loading her groceries at the Willow Mart, had invited her to sing with the Benders.

"Pretty flattering!" Marge reached for a mug. "He said he thought I was the torchy type and they wanted to try a bit of jazz in the mix."

Gracie laughed. "It's another of those occasions when experience trumps callow youth. I'm just surprised that Chad realized it. He already has Ashley, and Amy, too, to call on."

"Well, even if I don't quite understand it myself, I think bringing the kids' band in is one of the best things that's happened recently at Eternal Hope. We're having a lot of fun, aren't we?"

Gracie nodded her enthusiastic agreement. "Darla's promised to come on Sunday to hear Ashley and I think Jess Horton and her kids are coming, too," she added.

"Speaking of which, what's with all the mysteries? Are they solved?"

Gracie scrunched up her nose. "I'm praying each one solves itself. But Jess has a new problem. And it's more a menace than a mystery. I think she's got an unwelcome new neighbor—a guy who thinks he has a right to the profits from her late husband's research."

"Can't she call the police?"

"And charge him with what? Looking at real estate? He hasn't actually done anything, yet."

"What can we do?"

Gracie eyed her friend. "What do you mean, we?"

"Sherlock Parks and Marge Watson—or do you prefer Dr. Lawrence?"

"The trouble is, I'm not even sure yet that it's the same guy. But *someone* not from anywhere around here is considering buying the vacant place right across the street from Jess, and this Walter Blackstock has been in town, threatening Jess."

"So talk to Darla Knight. Get her on your side, now that you say you've got her coming to church."

Gracie smiled at the wisdom in that. "Darla helping Jess might just be restitution enough. You're great, Marge dear! Let's go and pay a visit to Darla. It's best to act while the inspiration's hot!"

"Before you think of a reason not to, is what you mean!" Marge teased her friend.

"Gracie Parks and company on the case!" She went on. "A little crime on the side adds a soupçon of excitement to the menus of any caterer!"

Darla's office was in a small building at the edge of town. Gracie recognized Roberta Ebersole behind the reception desk and greeted her. "I missed you at the Ecumenical Luncheon," Gracie told her.

The wife of the minister at Waxmire Tabernacle had an extraordinary voice, one that even Estelle admired. Roberta's perfect arias had cost Eternal Hope's choir first place in many a local competition.

"I had the chicken pox, believe it or not." Roberta laughed. "Horrible! It's a big deal when you're past middle age. I think I picked it up from one of the kids in the church nursery."

"I hear it's going round," Gracie said, thinking of the Horton kids. "Thankfully, I had it about a thousand years ago!"

Marge chuckled. "And I got them compliments of one Arlen Parks. I can sympathize with you, Roberta. Just remembering causes me to shudder."

"But what can I do for you all? Neither of you is selling a house, are you?"

"We came to see Darla Knight."

Roberta glanced toward the woman's office. "She's with Jim Thompson right now."

Gracie looked curiously at Roberta, who grimaced. "I think it's police business. Let me see how long she'll be."

Gracie and Marge waited while Roberta tapped on the door, then entered. It looked like Darla had been crying. Jim stood to greet them. Gracie glanced between the two of them, perplexed.

Without any preliminary small talk, Darla issued a dramatic statement, "Before you welcome my daughter and me into your church, you might as well know the whole sordid truth."

The police officer's expression was sympathetic. "You love Ashley. We can't fault you for that."

Darla sat behind her desk and arranged the already tidy files in front of her. "I guess, first things first. What can I help you ladies with today?"

"Our business can wait," Gracie said. She smiled at Darla who looked back defiantly.

"Well, then I can tell you that Jim here came to talk to me about a little problem I had and ended up sharing the Gospel." She forced a smile, tears suddenly welling in her eyes. "I tried to bribe the shop owner at the mall to drop the charges against Ashley."

Marge's eyes widened. Gracie said nothing.

"I know, it was incredibly stupid." Darla turned to Gracie. "What's worse is that this is the second time I've used *borrowed* funds on her behalf. But what I've done, or attempted to do, is no secret anymore. I'll let Officer Thompson explain."

Gracie looked at Jim.

"I got a call from the shop owner. Nice lady, goes to the same Bible study as my wife. She's beside herself. She already felt bad about pressing charges, but considered it the kind of tough love that might do Ashley good. Then, when Darla showed up, trying to get her to change her mind with the help of a little cash, she was upset. She didn't want to make things worse for the Knights, but she felt she needed professional advice. So she called me."

Ashley, it seems, had been shoplifting since before Darla and her husband had gotten their divorce. "Things were terrible," Darla told them. "We tried to keep it from Ashley, but she knew. We'd fight long into the night. Sometimes when I passed her room, I heard her crying. I should have done something then, but I couldn't think straight.

"My husband's business was growing, but not fast enough to pay all my bills. Ashley obviously inherited my gene for wanting things she can't afford. The first time, she took a T-shirt I wouldn't buy for her. She was only nine. I dismissed it as childish.

"A few months ago, she took a designer jacket from an expensive boutique. I paid them the money—it was almost six hundred dollars!—so they wouldn't press charges. Wes was accusing me of badmouthing his new wife to Ashley, and was being purposely slow with the child support, so I did the only thing I could think of—I borrowed the money from the club."

Darla paused, collecting her thoughts, struggling with her emotions. "I guess I felt I had to make up for what Wes and I had done. Poor Jess, she was the fall guy. I was desperate."

Gracie shook her head. "Well, now that you've told us, you don't have to be desperate any longer. And, the good news is, even before all this is settled, I have an idea how you can start making it up to her now. Jess *needs* help, and I think you might best be able to provide it."

Darla met Gracie's gaze. "I'll do anything, I swear, to make up for what I did."

"You have a client looking at the Horton house?"

"Walter Blackstock. He's from Rochester—a venture capitalist. He was here on business and decided Willow Bend is close enough to Chicago that, someday, it could be commuting distance."

"I hope that's not the case," Gracie replied. "I like us just the way we are. But regardless, I don't think that's actually why he's looking at properties here."

She filled Darla in on what she knew, and also on what she suspected. "I was hoping you could tell him that particular property has been sold. If I don't miss my guess, he'll quickly lose his interest in any other ones."

"It's not the most profitable way to do business—to take unsold houses off the market, right under the nose of an eager buyer, but . . . I'll call him this instant. It's the least I can do . . . for a start!"

GRACIE HAD JUST RETURNED from Darla's office when she heard the phone ring. Her inclination was to let the answering machine take the message, but something prompted her to listen. She picked up just in time to hear Jess say, "Gracie—"

"Hello?"

There was a soft sigh on the other end of the line. "Thank goodness you're home! I'm at the hospital."

Gracie felt her chest tighten. "Oh, dear Lord, no!"

"It's not like that—everyone is okay. The kids are fine."

Gracie sank into the chair beside the phone, and Gooseberry jumped into her lap. She rubbed his neck, as Jess poured out the story.

Walter Blackstock had stopped by to tell Jess that he was going to buy the house across the street from her. They got into an argument on the front porch, which Bobby apparently overheard from the sandbox nearby.

The sandbox happened to be close to a leftover pile of bricks from the backyard patio. Bobby, seeing his mother obviously upset, decided to take matters into his own hands, and heaved a brick at Walter, hitting him on the the side of his head. Walter stumbled forward, dazed, but conscious. Jess called Marilyn to watch the kids, and then took her husband's one-time partner to the hospital.

"He's got a lump the size of a grapefruit," Jess told her, "and there may be a slight concussion. The doctor is with him now. They sent us out to wait, so I called you."

"I'll come right over."

"No, Gracie, that's not necessary. Paul is with me. He was leaving the hospital as we were coming in. He was visiting someone from your congregation—a woman who was having cataract surgery, I believe."

Gracie silently thanked God for Paul.

"He's been great. He even put Walter at ease right away, taking charge with the admitting nurse, and getting all the paperwork filled out. He seems to know everyone in the hospital on a first-name basis!"

Gracie smiled, picturing her young minister greeting everyone familiarly the way he did at church each Sunday morning. "He has a knack for putting folks at ease, that's for sure."

Jess attempted a chuckle. "I didn't know what to say to Walter. I felt so humiliated by what Bobby had done!"

"Jess, I know how terrible this seems—it's an awful experience. But your son was only trying to protect his mother. Walter must have seemed like he was going to *harm* you!"

"I was so frightened before," Jess sighed, "but now it's in a different way."

"Where's Paul now?"

"I don't know how I would've handled the last hour without him." Jess apparently had not heard her question. "We drove most of the way in silence, with an occasional muffled moan from Walter. I knew you need to keep a person with a concussion alert! I was afraid he'd slip into a coma or something! I just babbled on about the weather, the traffic, the cars in the parking lot. I was still going a mile a minute when we ran into Paul. He calmed me down."

"Where is Paul now, dear?"

"Getting us some coffee." Then she changed the subject. "Oh, Gracie, what if Walter presses charges? Would he be so determined to get at me, that he'd take advantage of a little boy's mistake?"

Gracie hoped not. But then, he'd been willing to buy a house to harrass Jess and put silent pressure on her. He might be capable of anything!

"Is Paul going to see you home?"

"We both have cars here," Jess said, as though just realizing it herself. "I guess I'll drive myself. I'm okay, really. I'm staying until we know for sure that Walter is all right. And Paul offered to take him back to the Tourist Home."

Gooseberry looked up, concerned only with himself and the fact that, in her concern, Gracie had stopped stroking him.

She scratched his ears. "It's okay," she told him softly.

"Thank you, Gracie," Jess said, answering for the cat.

"Here's what I suggest," Gracie now said. "Marge can bring me over to the hospital and I can drive you home."

Eventually, Jess agreed to that.

"Gracie," she began again softly. "Will you please call Darla Knight for me? She left a message on my answering machine that she was planning to stop by today, but I'm just not up to it right now."

"Of course you're not." Gracie decided not to mention that she might know the reason for the call, and about Darla's change of heart.

Was it too much to hope that the brick knocked some sense into the man?

Gracie looked to heaven expectantly.

Walter was bandaged and ready to be discharged when Marge and Gracie arrived at the hospital. He sat in a wheelchair, silent and unreadable. Gracie greeted him with her warmest smile, for Jess's sake. Paul sounded more like a doctor than a preacher as he updated her. Walter, it had turned out, possibly had suffered a slight concussion. "But the doctor says it's nothing a strong painkiller and rest won't take care of."

Paul gazed protectively at his newest charge. "Mrs. Fountain will fix you right up with hot tea and toast. I called her and she's waiting for us."

"I'd appreciate your taking me to get my car—it's parked across the street from—" He glanced at Jess, who was standing off to the side, watching anxiously.

Paul interrupted. "Your car will be fine until tomorrow. You're not to drive—or do anything else—for at least twenty-four hours. The doctor wants to see you if anything changes."

"I'm missing my cell phone," Blackstock said, patting his pocket. "It's probably in her car, or on the porch. I need it. I've got business to take care of."

"I'll look for it," Jess offered timidly.

Paul took the handles of the wheelchair. "Phone calls can wait. Right now, I'm taking you where you can get some rest. You don't need to make things worse. Any business will keep until tomorrow."

Darla had, in fact, already relayed to Blackstock the news that the house was no longer available. It was Rocky who reported this to Gracie when he showed up at her back door later that night. He said that he'd run into Darla on the street and questioned her about the pending deal for the house across from the Hortons. She confided in him that she had, at Gracie's suggestion, lied to Blackstock, telling him that the bungalow was sold.

"She claims he took it well. He even offered to take her out to dinner, and pay her for her time and research. As a matter of fact," Rocky said, "she'd been planning to meet him this evening. I wonder if we should call her?"

Gracie cut Rocky a thick slice of the banana bread she'd baked to take her mind off the situation with the Hortons and the Knights and the Nickolsons. Not to mention Walter Blackstock's condition.

"*Umm*, smells delicious!" he said receiving the plate from her. "I'm starved!"

"What about all those nice groceries we bought you?" She eyed him. "Don't tell me you left them in the refrigerator to spoil!"

He gave a sheepish grin.

"Rocco Gravino!"

"I ate a bowl of cereal this morning, Gracie. I even put milk on it! Come on, give a guy a break! It's been a hectic day. Hammie popped in with a sample of the kind of nostalgia page he was talking about. We spent half the morning going over it."

"I hope you're going to incorporate Uncle Miltie's idea, as well."

"Have to." Rocky rolled his eyes. "Hammie loves it! And he's footing the bill on this page. It will take a couple of months to do the research in the *Gazette* archives just to collect enough photographs and news for the first few issues. What I was hoping is that Jess could work on this project— once she gets her life in order, that is."

"I think she will now," Gracie responded, thinking that Bobby's brick-throwing would certainly create ripples "I think she recognizes that running away from one's problems isn't a solution. Retreating from the fray doesn't work. And I think, she's finally realized that she's got friends, good friends, here in Willow Bend."

"And what about Ms. Knight? I don't know how you did it, but she seems suddenly a different woman."

She filled him in on what had happened with Jim at the real estate office.

"Darla was unusually friendly when I saw her." Rocky retained some skepticism. "She told me that Blackstock's actually not such a bad fellow. I had a hard time believing it, but Darla's proof, I guess, that people are never as they appear. She claimed he was even a bit flirtatious. I tell you, she seemed to relish sharing that."

Gracie laughed. "She's a pretty woman."

"If you like your dames cold and calculating," Rocky said.

She shook her head, her expression imploring him to give

Darla the benefit of the doubt. "So why do you suppose Blackstock went to see Jess, if Darla told him the property wasn't available anymore?"

"A last-ditch attempt, probably."

"It's hard to believe that he'd give up this easily."

Rocky said, "I took it upon myself to phone Dr. Samuels today. I thought I'd try to find out how much he knew about the situation."

"And?" Gracie urged him on.

"Turns out that he didn't know anything! Blackstock came to see him right after R. J.'s death. Samuels made it clear that they were a long way from securing a patent, and if and when they did, Blackstock had no claim on it."

She sipped her coffee, intrigued.

"Samuels said he threw the man out of his office because Blackstock got rude and threatened a lawsuit. One, I might add," Rocky said, "that won't hold up in court. I'm pretty certain of that."

Rocky went on to explain what Gracie already knew. Carroll Samuels had loved Jess and her husband like his own children. He'd promised to look out for R. J.'s interest in the research—which still was in the testing stages.

Gracie sighed, and stood. "What do you think Blackstock will do now?"

"Drop it. What else can he do?"

"Do you really think he's going to walk away with *nothing*—after coming all this way?"

"This guy lost money, so you can't blame him for wanting to get it back. He *seems* unscrupulous," Rocky conceded, "but, on the other hand, he does have his reputation to protect. Who's going to take a risk with him, if word gets out he's a crook? I figure he was ready to push Jess only so far—and now he's up against it. He has to cut his losses and move on."

"He thought he could bully Jess." And he'd almost succeeded!

"I'm sure Jess's husband wasn't this guy's only investment," Rocky was saying. "He makes his living taking risks. And a pretty good one it is, by what I've been able to glean."

Gracie glanced at Gooseberry, perched on his favorite spot on the windowsill to watch the birds. She called him down for a saucer of milk.

"This is all just the cost of doing business for Walter Blackstock. You win some, you lose some. That's the way venture capitalism is played, Gracie." He stood up to put his plate in the dishwasher.

Gracie leaned against the counter, attempting to sort it all out in her mind. Jess had let Blackstock scare her. It hadn't protected her, to have run away to Willow Bend. He had turned up, counting on her either to flee again or to give him what he wanted.

"I hope you're right," she thought out loud, "and that Blackstock really gives up. That he doesn't make trouble for Jess and little Bobby out of malice."

Rocky faced her. "Even if he does, Gracie, what's going to happen? Bobby's just a kid. What judge is going to fault a little boy for protecting his mom? Nobody here in Willow Bend, that's for sure."

Willow Benders were a special breed, she had to agree.

At that moment, Uncle Miltie appeared in the kitchen doorway. "What's there to eat?"

"Aren't you ever full?" Gracie teased.

The old man grinned. "Never!"

"How's the contraption on the roof performing?" Rocky shook his fist. "I'm ready to take it on again if the reception is still bad. What's another broken leg in a good cause?"

Uncle Miltie chortled. "Hah! You broke nothing except your promise to get it done in under an hour! But it was worth all your time . . . and injury—we've got channels all the way from Saturn, practically."

"You mean, now the science fiction movies you watch star real aliens!" Rocky teased him.

"I mean the cooking shows we get are full of cake recipes that need to bake for a couple of thousand light years!"

"Speaking of baking, would you fellows like some more of my banana bread?" Gracie asked.

"That sure a-peels to me," said Uncle Miltie, winking at them.

Gracie and Rocky looked at him affectionately.

"I'm too tired to groan," said Rocky.

"Ditto," Gracie concurred.

GRACIE WAS CHECKING OFF items on her errand list. Glancing at her watch, she decided to swing by the Nickolsons' house. *I miss rocking babies, Lord. Couldn't You persuade Arlen and Wendy to have another—a sweet little girl, while You're at it—if You don't mind!*

Katie sat next to Laura on the porch stoop, with their backpacks and scattered papers around them. Katie was punching numbers on a little calculator, while Laura scribbled on a pad

"Ah, genius at work," Gracie exclaimed, greeting them each individually. "Looks like algebra."

Laura slipped the pencil behind her ear. "Advanced algebra."

"We've got a test tomorrow," Katie added.

Gracie smiled, remembering how Arlen had kept a pencil behind his ear, and always one or two others in the pocket protector that matched the one his father used.

El used to worry about the boy, saying that during his teen years he'd seemed fonder of math than girls. Gracie assured him that their handsome son would bloom in his own good time. And he had: their sophomore year in college, shy Arlen had met Wendy.

Wendy and El had hit it off right away, but Gracie had had that old rhyme chafing at her heart: "A son is a son 'til he takes a wife. . . ."

Thank goodness for her own mother-in-law! She'd always treated Gracie like a daughter. "Make her the daughter of your heart, Gracie," Elmo's mother had advised. "You'll keep them close for life."

"A daughter's a daughter for all of her life," Gracie thought out loud.

"Mrs. Parks?" Katie was expecting an answer to a question Gracie hadn't heard.

She felt herself blush. "Forgive me, dear, for reminiscing. My son used to love algebra. He'd spend warm afternoons like these on the front porch doing his homework. I was just remembering."

"Mom and Dad aren't here," Katie announced with a pleased smile. "They're out on a date. Terry was going to take back that knife, and then they were going to get some ice cream."

Laura held up the baby monitor. "We're baby-sitting—cool, huh? This is my first job."

"Mine, too." Katie beamed. "Terry said that it was about time I earned my keep." Her eyes sparkled. "What he really meant was that he trusted me."

Gracie basked in Katie's happiness. But, after a moment, she told them sadly, "I guess I won't get to hold that adorable brother of yours today, since he's sleeping."

Katie's braces flashed. "We'll call you when he wakes up. You can hold him after you change his dirty diaper."

The girls broke into a fit of giggles.

"That's a police car," Laura said, pointing to the cruiser zipping by. She ran out to watch its route and reported back: "It looks like it's headed toward my house. . . ."

Or the Hortons's! Gracie excused herself.

"We want to go with you," Laura told her.

Gracie glanced at the kitchen door. Darren was inside asleep.

"You go," Katie said. "I'll stay with him."

Laura sat back down. "Friends, remember? We're in this together. So, back to business!" She looked to Gracie. "You'll call if there's a problem, right?"

Gracie nodded.

"Mr. Thompson was driving, so everything's going to be all right." Laura smiled at Katie, who grinned at her friend.

Gracie agreed. She had been impressed with all of Jim Thompson's involvement in the case to date. He'd acted out of concern and compassion; too bad she couldn't say the same for Walter Blackstock.

Bobby led Gracie into the living room, where Jess held Molly on her lap. She smiled and offered Gracie a seat. Katie had guessed well. Jess seemed in better spirits than Gracie had seen her in weeks. Jim Thompson stood to greet Gracie.

"You have better reception than that police scanner of mine. Herb always says so, and he's right."

Gracie explained that she'd spotted the cruiser while visiting the Claytons.

"Well, Blackstock isn't pursuing the matter. Seems even our 'villain' has a heart. The kid was only protecting his mom."

Jess hugged her son. "My hero!" she said.

"You got yourself quite a bodyguard here," Jim said.

He smiled at Gracie. "But I don't think I had as much effect as Darla Knight on his change of heart. If I don't miss my guess, he's finding a certain real-estate agent as desirable as her listings."

"Is he going back to New York?" Jess asked. "That's what I'd really like to know."

"I think so," Jim replied.

Jess looked relieved. "It's hard to think of him taking more than a business interest in Darla. But if he is, then maybe I can worry about him a lot less."

"There's something else you need to know," Gracie told her gently. "Darla Knight told Blackstock that the house had already been sold. And that misrepresentation will cost her a sizable commission."

Jess stared, dumbstruck.

At the risk of betraying too much in front of the children, Gracie added, "And the club's deficit has been returned."

Jess held up her hands. "I don't understand."

"All you need to understand is that Darla is another one of us who's on your side now." Gracie put her arm around Jess's shoulder and gave a squeeze.

Molly snuggled up against them both, and Gracie looked down at the little girl with a special, secret expression on her face.

"Me, too!" piped up Bobby, and they all laughed.

19

IN FACT, WALTER BLACKSTOCK did remain around Willow Bend for a few weeks, looking at speculative property. Most everyone figured he was actually more interested in matters of the heart than matters of real estate, and he actually turned up in church a couple of weeks later at Darla's side.

If the research went as well as Carroll Samuels was anticipating, R. J. Horton's work would soon be paying off, posthumously. Dr. Samuels's intention was to share fairly all proceeds with R. J.'s widow and children.

The Kidnappers Club finally did start to work harder to combine fiscal responsibility with fellowship. Moreover, they mended all their differences, welcoming one returning member, Marilyn Clayton, and two new ones, Marge and Gracie.

"I heard Darla's thinking of relocating," Estelle told Gracie, as they arrived for the first Saturday evening special service. "I guess Mason County is a little too small for her ambitions."

Gracie decided not to comment. Darla and Ashley had been coming to the late service every Sunday, and it seemed that the two were growing closer. Human beings were a complicated bunch, that was for sure.

She smiled at Estelle.

"Have you seen Paul?" Jess said, joining them for a moment at the back of the church.

"You two are getting pretty close," Estelle observed.

Jess laughed. "He's asked me about chaperoning a youth trip."

Perhaps—just perhaps—a romance would blossom one day between the two but, in the meantime, Gracie knew enough about gardening to protect a tender bud. She rescued Jess by putting the heat good-naturedly back on Estelle.

"Good chaperones are hard to find. What do you say we volunteer, Estelle?"

"Gracie, even I know you're teasing me! What if I take you up on it?" Estelle was actually twinkling.

"I'd think we were truly blessed. So much is changing in the world, Estelle. Young people need a church family to help them keep their bearings."

"Gracie!" Marge exclaimed, as she came up beside them. "What do you think? Estelle, I'm *not* asking *you*!"

Gracie eyed her friend quizzically. Marge was dressed in a sleek black dress, one in which only she could look so well. A flashy copper metallic scarf adorned her waist and draped triangularly across one hip.

Gracie could only shake her head. Estelle raised an eyebrow.

Marge spun around to give them the whole effect. "The band and I are doing a jazz medley of old gospel tunes tonight. We've been practicing for days!"

Gracie stood, pleased as punch with the developments, as her choir mates scurried to take their places.

"A penny for your thoughts?" It was her pastor beside her.

She smiled. "You did a good job."

"We all did." Paul smiled.

"Jess was looking for you."

"She found me. She's reading the Scripture lesson tonight."

That, more than anything else, pleased Gracie. "She said something about you two chaperoning the upcoming youth service trip."

"We're looking to be good friends for the long haul—who knows about anything else?" Paul's expression was pleased.

She only nodded, swallowing a satisfied chuckle.

Rocky now entered the church with Abe. They headed in the direction of Gracie, who waved them toward the pews.

"Break a leg, Gracie!" Abe called.

"Maybe in church, it's a wing," she heard Rocky correct him.

She sighed happily. It was time to head to the choir loft herself. The service would be starting soon.

Gracie had heard it said that the church was only one generation away from extinction. Yet, from her vantage point, as she entered the sanctuary, young people were almost all she could see.

Your church is safe with them, Lord. We lift up our voices together and we sing Your praises. Soft and loud, we blend our music to make one joyful noise. Old enemies are new friends—she saw Walter Blackstock seated next to Darla who was beside Jess Horton; Katie Nickolson was enfolded in the arms of both Phyllis and Terry; Uncle Miltie winked at her—*and Your goodness and grace are all-pervading.* She winked back.

And the band began to play.

Gracie's Banana Bread

- ✓ 1 cup sugar
- ✓ 1/2 cup oil
- ✓ 2 eggs
- ✓ 3 mashed (medium-sized) bananas
- ✓ 1/2 cup cottage cheese
- ✓ 1 teaspoon vanilla
- ✓ 1/2 teaspoon pumpkin pie spice
- ✓ 1 1/2 cups all-purpose flour
- ✓ 1 teaspoon baking soda
- ✓ 1/2 teaspoon salt

Preheat oven to 350 degrees F. Grease and flour just the bottom of a 9" × 5" loaf pan. Beat together sugar and oil in a large bowl. Add the eggs, well-mashed bananas, cottage cheese and vanilla. Mix together well.

Add pumpkin pie spice, flour, baking soda and salt. Stir until just blended, with all ingredients moistened.

Pour into the loaf pan and bake for an hour, or until a skewer inserted into the center of the loaf comes out clean.

Cool for five minutes before removing from pan.

Gracie says, "Uncle Miltie likes to call this my 'pan-ana bread.' That's because I often take banana bread slices and brown them lightly in butter in a cast-iron frying pan. Add a little maple syrup and you have a new version of breakfast French toast. Add a scoop of vanilla ice cream and it's dessert!"

About the Author

"I, like Gracie, love homemaking and cooking," writes ROBERTA UPDEGRAFF. "I married my high-school sweetheart, have been married for more than twenty-five years and have three-plus wonderful children. I say *plus* because our home seems to sprout teenagers and young adults, making our dinner table banter quite lively. This year we will host our second exchange student, and we've just returned from a lovely reunion with his predecessor, our new Italian son.

"I am a substitute teacher at Williamsport High School in Pennsylvania, and I love my students! I have taught everything from auto mechanics to orchestra. I am also a Sunday school teacher and volunteer youth leader. I enjoy teenagers.

"We continue our families' tradition by serving God as volunteers in mission. This summer we will return to Honduras for the fourth time to help with the ongoing reconstruction after Hurricane Mitch. In August 2001, our whole family served in Honduras together. My husband joined us after completing the five-thousand-mile trip from Pennsylvania to Honduras in the small school bus we called *La Pequeña Mula*. He donated the bus and contents on behalf of our presbytery.

"I am a member of the St. David's Christian Writers' Conference board of directors, and I am active in West Branch Christian Writers. This is my fourth book in the 'Church Choir Mysteries' series, and I continue to write for publications like *Moody*, *Focus on the Family* and *Group Magazine*."